Katie L. Carroll

Paperback ISBN: 978-1-958575-14-7
Ebook ISBN: 978-1-958575-15-4

Cover and interior design by Shimmer Publications

Shimmer Publications LLC
Milford, CT

Visit the author's website at www.katielcarroll.com

To those of you surviving...
May you find a way to truly live.

CHAPTER 1

The hens flocked to the pieces of homemade cornbread Mel tossed into the pen. A loud bluish-gray one, who Mel had dubbed Rachel Lynde, flapped her wings and scattered the others so she had first pick of the food.

Once Rachel Lynde was occupied, a mottled silver-and-black hen named Marilla led the rest to breakfast. The wispy orange one—Anne Shirley, naturally—meandered over last, her beak pointed to the sky as if imagining shapes in the puffy clouds above. When little Minnie May hopped too close to Rachel Lynde, the bigger hen pecked at her.

"Settle down, girls," Mel said. "There's plenty for everyone."

Not to be ignored, a rooster let out a robust cock-a-doodle-doo from his solitary pen adjacent to the henhouse.

"Plenty for you, too, Mr. Gilbert Blythe." In went a portion of cornbread for Gilbert.

It had been Gilbert who originally alerted Mel to the chickens' existence. She had been riding her bike around, scavenging for firewood, when she'd heard the distinct crow of a rooster. The flock was was somehow still alive, though it must have been at least a year since anyone had taken care of them.

Mouth agape, Mel had stared at them for a full five minutes before coming to her senses. The fence that kept the animals penned in was attached to a shed. The doors were open, and there was a dwindling supply of chicken feed inside. The bags were piled high, all of them sliced open. The feed had spilled out in a scattered mess. All but one bird had survived. Mel surmised that the last act of one of the farmers had been providing this feast, a dying person's parting gift for the chickens.

The next day, she visited the library and procured a book about raising chickens. Then, she began gathering materials to build a pen on her cabin property. Buckets of sweat and one swollen thumb later—Mel wasn't great with a hammer—she had a new home for the flock. It was a comedy of errors to get the birds in cat carriers and bike them up to the cabin one-by-one, but in the end, she made it happen.

An impatient caw pulled Mel from her reverie. A murder of crows sat patiently on the branches of a tall pine tree. The caw was the friendly kind, not the panicked squawk that warned of predators. The crows were far less rowdy than the hens.

Mel clicked her tongue in greeting and scattered the rest of the cornbread among the pine needles at the base of the tree. One-by-one the crows swooped down for breakfast.

Warm mug of tea in hand, Mel yawned and took in the mountain view beyond the trees. The sky above was clear except for a few fair weather clouds, but the morning mist stubbornly clung to the mountain peaks. She stole one last look at the view. It was the kind of scene she wished she had someone to share it with.

Despite her jacket and the warm tea, she shivered, a reminder that spring could be slow to come to upstate New

York.

No frost this morning, at least. A solid week had passed since the last frost, which meant it was safe to begin planting some of the more tender seeds and seedlings. There was a lot to do this spring and no one to do it but Mel.

Spring was planting season. The earth thawing. Sowing seeds. New life sprouting after a long winter. Each tiny tendril hope incarnate.

She clicked her tongue one last time at the birds. It was the most interactive part of her day, done and over with.

"There's no point in wallowing," she chided herself as she returned her mug to the cabin and gathered the seeds from the pantry and the gardening tools from the shed.

Wallowing only made the wave of loneliness harder to shake off. It had been about five years since Mel had seen another human being. Well, since she'd seen another *living* human being, but she didn't like to think about that.

She wasn't exactly counting the days, though she was counting sunflower seeds as she dipped her gloved fingers into the rich soil to make holes. She kept a calendar, so it wasn't hard to do the math. The calendar helped her keep track of planting and harvesting times. A vitally important skill when you were the only person left in the world.

To be fair, Mel didn't have definitive proof that she was the sole person to have survived the pandemic to end all pandemics. But it had been nearly five years since she had permanently relocated to the mountain cabin and nary another human soul to be found.

Hopes of meeting a real, live person in the flesh had dwindled away as the days had passed, until hope had all but disappeared. If anyone had survived in all of North America, they had yet to make their way to Mel's place. And she figured they never would. If there were any survivors, they were likely too far away and occupied with their own survival to make it to her humble abode. She was well on her way to assuming she was the last person alive.

She supposed there could be another survivor on the far side of the country...or the world. Mel imagined a resilient soul in California picking grapes by day and strumming a guitar by night. The soloist of solos. Or perhaps there was an intrepid soul in India who grew their own curry ingredients and collected rainwater for the crops.

Mel was lucky enough to have a steady supply of water from a well with a solar pump. It was one aspect of survival she was allowed to take for granted. Though now that she thought of it, collecting rainwater wasn't a bad idea. If she got done with her chores early enough, she could ride her bike down to the library to see if there were any books on the subject.

Mel continued to dig holes and count seeds as she absentmindedly hummed a tune, the chickens clucking in their pen and the wind chimes hanging on the cabin porch her accompaniments.

Before long, she grew warm enough to take off the jacket. Once the rows of sunflowers seeds were planted and Mel had recorded it in her notebook, she filled a watering can and gave them a good drink.

She sighed and wiped her dirty hands on her jeans. The denim had once been stiff and sturdy, but they were getting a little threadbare in the usual places, mainly in the area where her thighs met her butt. Unlike the denim, her joints were the stiffest they had ever been. As a kindergarten teacher, she had spent many days getting up and down on the floor, but now that she was in her mid 40s, her knees popped whenever she crouched.

A crow watched from one of the wooden posts Mel had

hammered into the ground to support the sunflower plants once they were fully grown. Putting the posts in before the seeds might have seemed premature, but Mel liked to be prepared. Plus, it had given her something to do while waiting for the risk of frost to pass. Spending the early spring days preparing meant that now she could devote all her time to growing. Abundant crops were necessary for survival.

From its perch, the crow flapped its wings, a tear evident in one of them.

"Oh, hello, Tiny Tim," she said.

Unlike the chickens, who all had names, this crow was the only one Mel had given one to. As a baby, it had been attacked by a hawk. Mel had watched the big crows charge at the predator, chasing it into the sky until the hawk dropped the baby.

In a feat she still wasn't sure how she managed to pull off, Mel had run across the yard to catch the little crow. She'd then made a blanket nest at the base of the pine tree and watched as the big crows crowded around the baby, caring for it until it grew big enough to fly on its own. The tear in the wing was a reminder of how harsh nature could be.

She supposed it was a little unhinged to anthropomorphize the crows and chickens the way she did, clicking her tongue to get their attention and chatting with them when they stopped by. Would it be worse to only have herself to talk to? Yes, it would be infinitely worse.

It was a stroke of luck the birds hadn't been affected by the sickness that had wiped out humans, along with all the other mammals on the planet as far as Mel could tell. The chickens sustained her body with their eggs, and the crows sustained her lonely heart with their company.

Mel tried to count her blessings instead of hardships. She knew all too well how easy it was to get buried

underneath dark thoughts, so she opted to see the sunny side
if she could.

CHAPTER 2

After a morning of hard work, Mel decided she had earned that trip to the library she had been thinking about. In addition to looking for information about collecting rain water, she wanted to grab a few new fiction titles and look for books about breeding chickens.

Poor Josie Pye had passed away this winter. When Mel had first found the hen's body, she had been worried about an illness infecting the flock—a natural place for her mind to go in the after-times of the pandemic. But all of the other hens remained the picture of health through the rest of winter and into spring.

Mel had read the lifespan of a chicken was five to ten years, and those weren't all egg-producing years. She knew at some point, she'd have to breed the chickens in order to keep a supply of eggs. It pained her to think of losing any other hens or Gilbert, but such was the way of the world.

Mel retrieved one of her bikes from the shed. She had hauled two up here to make sure she had a back-up and spare parts. They were replicas of vintage bicycles, pilfered from a big box store. She had acquired them when the old pickup truck had still been running, knowing that wouldn't last forever.

Today, she chose the vibrant yellow bike. Its paint job had acquired a few chips with time, and the wide leather seat was worn with use. The charming mode of transportation was complete with a metal basket affixed in front of the handlebars. Between the basket and her large backpack, she had plenty of space for anything she would acquire in town.

In the beginning of her time at the mountain cabin, Mel had taken many rides in the truck to nearby towns and acquired many things. Now, the truck was more a lawn ornament than anything else, sitting in the dirt driveway where Mel had last left it. Wildflowers grew up along the side of it in the summer.

Aside from the supply trips, Mel hadn't traveled...save for one memorable road trip.

It was on the one-year anniversary of her husband's death, about eleven months since she had seen another living human. This was before she had her vegetable garden and her chickens. She had been living off of rations she had gathered, pillaging canned goods and other shelf-stable food from shops and grocery stores. She never took anything from people's houses if she could help it, if only to avoid the dead bodies as much as possible.

She and Daniel—her late husband—never had children, only their trusty dog, Bruno. But Mel was a kindergarten teacher, so each year had brought a whole classroom of five-year-olds to teach and nurture. Having nothing but herself to fret over for a year had grown torturously tedious. Everything in her life had felt stale, right down to the contents of the cans and jars in her kitchen. Even the summer mountain air had a musty quality to it that year.

One night she went to bed and couldn't sleep. An

overwhelming restless energy had possessed Mel. The next morning, eyes still wide open, she stared at the wooden beams in the ceiling, a wild idea possessing her. She hopped on the bike with no supplies except the clothes on her back until she found a hybrid car sitting in the driveway of a small ranch with an attached garage.

Ignoring her rule about breaking into houses, Mel first tried kicking in the front door with her heel, like some kind of action hero. When all that resulted in was a sore foot, she broke the window next to the door with a big stick. She cleared away the biggest shards of glass with the stick and carefully reached in to unlock the door from the inside.

She walked into a living room, the air stale and stuffy but not putrid. The inside of the house had that eerie stillness of every empty indoor place, a feeling Mel thought she would never get used to. She avoided looking down a hallway to the right where there were probably bedrooms and headed straight ahead to an eat-in kitchen with sliders out the back and a door to the left. Two key fobs hung neatly on hooks next to the door that probably led to the garage. She grabbed the one of the same make as the hybrid outside.

It took a few tries to get the car started, but once she did, she drove south on the country road until she reached the highway. No one else was on the road, of course, but she drove 65 miles per hour on the dot, using the cruise control to stick to the speed limit. It might have been a rush to punch the gas pedal all the way and push the sedan to its limits, but what would have been the point?

Mel had never been much of an adrenaline junkie. Even before they bought the cabin, she and Daniel would take a ski trip each winter break. Daniel would hit the double black diamond trails, and Mel would do a few runs on the green trails before calling it a day. She much preferred a spot by the fire in the big lodge, curled up with a book.

Even now with the bicycle, she walked it down the dirt driveway, skirting around rocks and weeds pushing up through the dirt, waiting to hop on the bike until she reached the paved road. She kept one hand engaged on the back break to keep her speed in check as she rode down the winding hill. The breeze blew her chestnut brown hair—admittedly, now peppered with a bit of gray—off her face. That was all the excitement she needed these days, the restlessness having long left.

It had felt like such a long time back then to have no interaction with another person. In that first year, she hadn't really gone out of the way to search the world to find any other survivors. After Daniel's death, she had gone deep into mourning, expecting to die herself and coming to terms with that. When she didn't die, life became a long slog of surviving on her own. As she scavenged for supplies, she hadn't come across any survivors, but she hadn't been looking either.

That anniversary had sparked something in her, a need to search. There was still some hope left that there were others back then. That desperate drive felt like a long time ago, though only four years had passed since then.

She was a very different person now than she had been. And she was living proof that you could live a life of simple joys even in the worst of circumstances.

CHAPTER 3

Tears prickled Mel's eyes as she coasted down the hill on her bike. She might have fooled herself into blaming the wind for the tears if she hadn't been thinking about the anniversary road trip.

Her philosophy on life had changed that day. Once she had made her way back home, she'd vowed to stop slogging through life and to take charge of surviving. That's when she started gardening, and a little while later, she'd found her chickens. The change had resparked her natural curiosity. Curiosity and learning were fundamental parts of her old self as a kindergarten teacher, and tapping into them to survive made her feel alive again.

She'd also worked on her ability to compartmentalize. Certain thoughts had certain boxes, some she kept closed and others she flung open as often as possible. Those deep, dark feelings were best kept locked up, so they couldn't overwhelm her again.

With that in mind, Mel firmly gripped the bike handlebars to steer herself straight and let the wind swipe away the tears on her cheeks. The fresh air worked its magic on her mood. The cool mountain breeze stung her face. Even with a helmet atop her head, the long tendrils of hair that had escaped whipped across her face.

Trees shadowed the edges of the road, but she kept to the middle where the sun shone down on her, warming her from the top down. She imagined it feeding her soul, her spirit lifting like the sunflower blooms following the path of the sun across the sky.

It was tempting to close her eyes, but the roads around here had never been in great shape. Seasons of water seeping into cracks, freezing, and melting were harsh on the asphalt surface. Weeds, too, thrived with no traffic to keep them at bay. So she kept her eyes on the road as she neared the end of the winding turns.

The road leveled off and the trees thinned, making way for something that felt more like civilization when civilization was still a thing. Mel pumped the pedals to keep a steady pace on the bike. She passed by all the familiar landmarks, fancy chalets for the rich, family-run inns, and less-expensive rental places. Time and disuse had given them all a weathered look, nature beginning to take them all for herself.

The Thirsty Crow Tavern marked the start of town and the end of the country road. Mel slowed and took a right at the intersection, the only one in town that had a stoplight. It used to blink on and off all day and night, but now it hung dark.

She passed by the gas station, dusty and overgrown with weeds, and rode over the small bridge that spanned the river, coming to a stop outside the library. She propped the bike on its kickstand on the sidewalk and hung the helmet from the handlebars. She fluffed out her helmet hair as she caught her breath from the vigorous ride.

The library building was an old Roman Gothic church made with brown stones. The windows were arched, and a small square steeple sprouted up on the left side. The right side of the church spilled into a more modern part that had been added on. The newer part was made of bricks that didn't quite match the original stonework. It was a rather unique look for a library, and a bit of a Frankenstein monster with modern conveniences pieced together with the original footprint.

The main entrance had a covered landing with staircases on either side, one of which had been retrofitted with a ramp. Mel skirted around the rather grand entrance and slipped into the library through an unassuming side door made of metal. It was painted brown to match the stones so it mostly blended in with the facade.

This put her right into the corner of a large room with high ceilings and stained-glass windows. There were tables and chairs set up in the middle of the space with shelves of books in the back and front. A catwalk with even more shelving ran around the perimeter of the room, accessed by a metal staircase on one side and a ramp on the other.

On sunny days like today, light poured in through the stained-glass windows, painting the library in a kaleidoscope of colors.

She sighed and then breathed in the scent of books. She loved this library.

Mel would've liked to transport all the books up to her home. Well, maybe not all the books—she wasn't much into legal thrillers and horror stories gave her nightmares, something you didn't want to have when you were all alone on a very dark mountain every night—but many of the books. There was nowhere for her to store a library's worth of books, though.

The cabin was full of food, seeds, and herbs, and her shed was for various supplies. Among the many items in there, she had what she calculated to be a lifetime's worth of cotton socks. Plus, the shed wasn't climate controlled, so not a good fit for books even if she had the space. Not that the library was climate controlled these days, but the inside was better protection from the elements than her shed.

Mel had settled on keeping the most important books at home all the time, mainly those about growing and making the things she needed for everyday life, along with a few of her favorites. In the warmer months, she rotated other books in and out of her personal collection with regular trips to the library. The fantasy and romance sections saw heavy usage. Before the winter months came, she would always stock up on books in case the weather prevented her from riding down the mountain road.

She loved picture books, too. But she didn't read those. Not anymore. Too many memories.

Today, she reshelved a dark fantasy romance and went in search of what to read next. It was a busy planting time, so she wanted to grab a few books in case she didn't make it back to the library for a couple of weeks. She selected a romance with an illustrated cover that looked light-hearted and a sci-fi that had a love story in it. Then, she headed to the fantasy section where she decided to randomly select books.

She picked a shelf, closed her eyes, and ran her fingers across the spines as she slowly walked down the aisle. She counted to seven—her favorite number—and grabbed whatever book her fingers were touching and slipped it into her bag without looking at the cover. She did this two more times, until she had three surprise fantasy books to read.

This was risky to do with fantasy because a lot of the

books were series and she might get a book that wasn't the first one. When that happened, she simply kept the book in her cabin and grabbed the rest of the series the next time she went to the library. It was the kind of risk that kept life interesting but didn't pose any real danger.

The nonfiction section was organized with the Dewey Decimal system. With no power, there was no computer system, and therefore no help in finding the subjects she desired. Originally, she had known very little about the numbering system, other than the biographies being in the 900 section, so this had initially presented itself as a challenge.

But now, she knew all the topics and their numbers. Today brought her to the 600 section. It was a well-perused one because it included the agricultural and health books, quite a few of which had a permanent home at the cabin. She was surprised to find several books on raising and breeding backyard chickens and one on rain collection systems. This was a bigger library when it came to rural communities, but it was still not what she would have considered large. Then again, it was a topic that could have been popular in this particular community, especially given how she had found her chickens not too far from there.

She added the books to her tote bag and decided she had better head home. Though sunset was hours away, she did not want to chance getting caught out in the dark. It was a much longer ride home up the hill than it was coming down.

CHAPTER 4

Mel's hands felt raw after a morning of laundry, even with wearing gloves, and she was soaked and shivering. She had always hated laundry. And having to do it by hand in water that turned cold way too fast...well, that had been a thing that had nearly sent her over the edge a few times in the last five years.

She settled for rewearing her clothes as much as she could stand and washing the laundry no more than once every two weeks. She got away with doing it even less in the winter when she didn't get sweaty working in the garden.

At least she hadn't had to make her own laundry detergent, not yet. The powdered detergent she had stocked up on seemed to last indefinitely, so long as she stored it where it stayed dry. She used maybe a teaspoon every time she did laundry.

She hoped it would be a long time before she had to find that detergent recipe in her notebook. It used ash of all things. Imagine something so messy cleaning laundry!

Mel hung her clean clothes, towel, and a handful of dish rags on the clothesline that ran from one end of the cabin to a sturdy tree. The clothesline, like the chicken coop, was one of her greatest triumphs that came at the cost of a sore thumb. It seemed whenever she used a hammer, she ended up with an injury—thankfully only minor ones so far.

After a quick snack of cold rosemary potatoes leftover from breakfast, Mel turned her attention to planting corn. It was one of the most important crops because she could make cornmeal with it. Properly-stored cornmeal lasted a year and was versatile. She could use it to make biscuits, cakes, pancakes, dumplings, muffins, pie crust, and so much more.

During the summer and most of the fall, Mel had a steady supply of fresh food. It was the winter and early spring that were the trickiest. She grew a few crops, like romaine lettuce, inside year-round, but not enough to sustain her through the cold months. Building a greenhouse was a pipe dream, and she shuddered thinking of the injuries she might sustain in tackling a project like that. Instead, she relied on drying, pickling, and long-storage methods to survive the winter.

As she planted the rows of corn seeds, Mel's thoughts wandered to her very first gardening project with one of her kindergarten classes. They had planted beanpole seeds and also zinnias in little paper cups. The kids brought them home as Mother's Day gifts.

Mel had planted her seedlings in her little yard at home. A few of them withered, but she had grown enough to make a couple of side dishes with the beans. In the summer, the zinnias had bloomed in a cheerful array of colors. It was like a tiny fireworks show in her garden, and the bees seemed to love them as much as she did.

After that school project, Mel had been hooked on growing things from seeds. It became a project her class did every year and sowed a love of gardening for a fair few of her students, some of whom had sent her pictures of their gardens years later.

A splotch of wetness hit her soil-covered glove. She blinked and let the tears fall. Grief over losing all those young lives was one of the boxes she usually kept closed. It did no good to linger on the losses, but it also wasn't good to repress them all the time. Planting corn seeds and remembering old students' gardens was a box she allowed herself to crack open, but not for long.

Soon, she wiped the tears away and went to get water from the hose. She held the end of the hose in the watering can and turned the spigot attached to the side of the cabin. Nothing happened. Not even a drop of water came out.

Mel turned the spigot to the closed position and then twisted it back open. Still no water.

Taking a deep breath to quell her shaking hands, she went inside and tried the kitchen tap, followed by the bathroom one. Both were as dry as a glue stick left open overnight by a kindergartner. Plenty of water had been available for the laundry this morning. So what was the problem now?

She bit her lip as a million thoughts swirled through her mind, most of them of the panicky variety. Fresh water was life. Her plants needed it to survive. Mel needed it to survive.

"Don't panic," she told herself.

She took another calming breath and trudged to the back of the property to the well and pump. An inspection of the solar panels showed nothing amiss. There had been a good rainfall just the other day, so it wasn't likely that the well had run dry. That meant the problem was the pump itself, the battery, or maybe one of the pipes.

Were there any other parts that Mel was missing? She

didn't really know that much about the system and how it all worked. Professionals had installed it the year she and Daniel had bought the cabin, and it had worked perfectly fine since then...until today.

Even if she could figure out what the problem was, would she be able to fix it?

There were other water sources nearby, like the river, but none so convenient as the well. The water system had been the one comfort she'd been allowed to take for granted. Water for cooking, cleaning, and drinking that was sent right into her cabin was no small miracle.

In a world where she worked so hard to stay alive, that single convenience was a lifeline. She imagined trudging through snow in the dead of winter to get to the river. Doing this day after day on top of all the other things she did. The thought was overwhelming.

Mel stared at her hands, caked with dirt, cracked with hard work. Despair gripped her. Her body shook with it. She had never wanted to feel this way ever again. The all-consuming grief that started in her chest and spread to every part of her, paralyzing her with its power. She had found her way out of it once, but she didn't think she could do it again.

"No," she whispered to her trembling hands. She said it over and over again, ending with one last primal scream. "No!"

The sound startled a roost of birds in the trees, and a plague of grackles burst into flight. Blurred in her teary vision, the birds' blue-black forms were a rushing river in the sky. They disappeared into the distance, leaving Mel alone in her desperate state.

She fell to her knees and sobbed into her dirty hands. Snot ran from her nose and sobs wracked her core, but she barely noticed. She barely even felt her body, so consumed with grief she was.

Freakish sounds of sorrow poured from her mouth. She cradled her head, pulled at her hair, and rocked up and down with primal screams.

Finally, she wore herself out and lay on her side next to the water pump system. She must have been a sight, her face a mess of dirt and snot, her hair a riot of curls around her head.

Through the ragged sound of the breath she was having trouble catching, came something she never thought she would hear again in her life.

Someone else's breath.

In a slight southern accent, that someone asked, "Ma'am, are you okay?"

CHAPTER 5

The voice startled her to her feet. She wiped her nose with the back of her hand, smearing it with snot, as she stared at a man. An actual living human being. In front of her.

Her mouth opened in a little "o," no words able to form.

The man had a short afro that was haloed by the sun like he was an angel. Mel didn't believe in angels, but at that moment, she would have believed this man flew down from the heavens. Where else would he have come from?

He took a step closer so the sun no longer shone directly behind him, and his features came into clearer focus. His skin was a rich umber, and his beard was black and fluffy but neat. His eyebrows were furrowed in concern above his dark brown eyes, the rest of his face set in a careful expression.

Mel wasn't very good at estimating people's heights—to be fair she hadn't seen a real, live person for a long time—so her brain simply informed her that he was quite tall. His broad shoulders and chest were burdened with many straps, most noticeably one that led to a rifle slung over his right shoulder and a second one that supported a guitar case on his left shoulder.

His hands were relaxed at his side in a non-threatening manner, and he kept what felt like a safe distance from her.

As startled as Mel was with this man's impossible appearance, she wasn't frightened. She wasn't excited, either. Her emotional outburst had wrung her dry of emotions. After the initial shock of hearing the stranger speak and seeing him for the first time, it was a sort of mild numbness that overtook her.

The man cleared his throat. "Are you okay?" he asked again.

"Uh," Mel managed to utter. "Yes...I mean, no. Well, I think my water pump is broken, which would be very bad, but I'm not hurt or anything."

She was rambling, and her gaze kept swiveling back and forth between the dysfunctional well system and the man, like she couldn't make heads or tails of either one. And, well, that was the truth of the matter. She didn't know what to make of any of this.

Maybe she had hit her head and was having some sort of concussed hallucination. Maybe she was sick in her bed and all of this was a fever dream.

Mel dug her thumb fingernail into the tip of her pointer finger. The nail pierced through the calloused skin, producing a dull pain that should have been confirmation that this wasn't a dream or hallucination, though she still couldn't quite believe her own eyes.

The man took one step closer and held out his right hand. Mel looked at her own hands in confusion as if they might be able to tell her what to do in response.

"I'm Jaylen," he said.

A handshake. He was holding his hand out for a handshake.

Mel moved toward him, her legs as slow and stilted as her mind. She held out her right hand but still wasn't close enough to reach his. He bridged the gap between them and grasped her hand. His was firm and warm, the skin dry and calloused like hers.

The human-to-human contact sent a jolt of energy across her skin that culminated in a prickling in her scalp. She'd forgotten what it felt like to touch another person. There'd been nights, both long ago and more recent, where she'd ached to be held, afraid she would fall apart from loneliness. Yet, this small touch felt almost too much to bear.

A second too late, she realized her hand was still moist with snot and tears. He didn't seem to notice, or he pretended not to. She hastily pulled it out of his grasp.

"Mel," she said, coming to her senses. "I'm Mel."

"Nice to meet you, Mel."

The man—Jaylen—smiled. It was the kind of smile that lit up his face, that lit up the world. It was so bright and genuine, she almost had to look away.

All at once, she was struck with the beauty of seeing another face. The brightness of his smile matched his eyes. He had a small dimple in one cheek but not the other. His was a handsome face, to be sure, but not strikingly so. Not a face that in the before-times would have stopped her thoughts in their tracks and distracted her so thoroughly.

The beauty lie in how animated it was. How utterly, beautifully alive it was.

Perhaps any face would have had the same effect after such a long time of not seeing one. Or perhaps not.

As Jaylen's face settled back into that thoughtful expression, the mesmerizing quality didn't lessen any. Mel couldn't stop staring and had a bizarre urge to reach up and caress his cheek.

It was all so surreal, having another person here in her backyard, that she couldn't figure out how to act around him.

"Where did you come from?" she asked. She half expected him to confess he was one of the fae folk, materialized from a mushroom in the forest. She waved the thought away; clearly, she'd been reading too much fantasy.

"I'm originally from Atlanta," he said matter-of-factly. "But my work brought me to D.C., and I've been living there since…well, since before everything happened."

There was no need to explain what he meant by that.

So, he was from Atlanta and lived in D.C., but that was in the before-times. What had he been doing since then? And what brought him here to her cabin in upstate New York?

Before she voiced any of these questions, Jaylen gestured to the well and pump system. "Can I take a look, ma'am?"

Mel shot him a glare. "Did you just ma'am me?"

She patted her head, frizzy hair sticking out of the ponytail she had corralled it into earlier. She didn't look in the mirror too often these days, though there was a small one in her bathroom above the sink. There was no reason to fuss over her looks. Who would care about the occasional gray hair or the wrinkles that had begun to crease her face? The crows and chickens made no such judgments.

Heat rose to her cheeks with the sudden bout of self-consciousness, a feeling that had become a stranger to her. But now she felt it keenly, and it made her wonder just how much of her brown hair was streaked with gray for this man to be calling her "ma'am."

"An old habit. No offense intended," Jaylen said with sincerity, though she detected a hint of a smile about his face. He set down his burdens, including the gun, and gestured again at the pump. "May I?"

"Sure, of course."

Mel stepped aside and resisted the urge to tidy her clothes. When she looked down at them, she quickly realized they were so disheveled as to be beyond fixing.

What was wrong with her? She hadn't been this discombobulated since the first time she wrangled Gilbert into his pen.

She blew out a loud breath that puffed the hair off her forehead.

Jaylen turned toward her with a smile that made her cheeks warm. "Everything alright?"

"Oh, yes," she said. "Perfectly fine."

Which was anything but the truth. There was nothing fine about all the strange feelings the appearance of this man was stirring up inside her.

CHAPTER 6

While Jaylen examined the pump equipment, it gave Mel a chance to gather her emotions and put them back into their respective boxes. And a chance to observe him.

He was definitely younger than she was, but by how much? His face was unlined, but that wasn't always a good indicator of age. His eyes held a depth and maturity to them that made her think he couldn't be more than ten years her junior. Perhaps the circumstances he had endured in these after-times gave his stare a gravitas that defied his years.

The fact was that her life was one of survival, and survival meant hard work. She was sure Jaylen's life was no exception to this. Again, she wondered what he had been doing these last five years, while also recognizing it wasn't any of her business.

Jaylen's deep voice interrupted her thoughts as he said, "The solar panels look fine."

That much she had already figured out.

"Did you install this yourself?" he asked.

"No. We had it installed by a company."

Her brow furrowed in consternation when she realized

she used the communal "we," including her late husband in the conversation. She hadn't been part of a "we" in a very long time. A detail that apparently hadn't escape Jaylen's notice.

"Does someone else live here with you?" he asked.

The question seemed innocent enough, though it made her rethink how much information to share with this man, who for all his novelty, was definitely a stranger. The idea of stranger danger had grown completely foreign to her, but it would behoove her to have a little of it right then.

She avoided the question. "Do you know a lot about water pumps?"

"Not specifically, but I'm pretty handy when it comes to building things."

"Are you a carpenter or a contractor or something?"

He stepped around her to get to his bags and poked around in one. "I'm an electrical engineer, but I mostly worked in the aerospace industry."

"Aerospace?" Mel shook her head in disbelief. "Like working on airplanes?"

"Yup." Jaylen produced a multi-tool from his bag. "Do you mind if I take a look in the control box?"

Mel shook her head. He got to work unscrewing the cover of the box.

She answered numbly as he asked her questions about the age of the system and how much water she typically used in a day. His voice faded away as she continued to wonder about how he had seemingly appeared from thin air to solve her very specific problem.

She went and stood right next to Jaylen, close enough to feel the heat of his body. It wasn't a particularly warm day. Mel had been shivering while doing the laundry, but a sheen of sweat covered Jaylen's forehead, and he wore only a t-shirt.

She breathed in his scent of earth and sweat, trying to find something to anchor her back to reality. He smelled real enough, but she couldn't quite believe in him yet.

She reached out a finger and poked his bicep.

"Uh." He looked at her, creases worrying his forehead. "Do you need something?"

"Oh." Mel's hands flew to her cheeks. They were ablaze with heat. "No. I just…"

She took a few steps back. What must he be thinking of her behavior?

The concerned look on Jaylen's face deepened. He removed the distance between them and gently gripped her upper arm as if to steady her. "Let me get you some water."

She peered into his deep brown eyes. "No, I'm okay."

"I insist. With your water supply not working, you're probably dehydrated."

He squeezed her shoulder before letting go and going back to his bag. As he rummaged through them, Mel turned her back for a moment and took a few deep breaths.

She had to get herself together. She was starting to feel a little light-headed and would never recover if she passed out from the simple fact of interacting with another human being, as unbelievable as it was after all this time alone.

"Here." Mel turned back around to find Jaylen holding out a stainless steel water bottle.

He had unscrewed the cap already, so she took the bottle and drank a small sip. It was surprisingly cool as it coated her mouth and went down her throat. And refreshing.

She hadn't realized how dry her mouth had grown, but she suspected that had more to do with the shock of meeting Jaylen than with dehydration. The water had been working fine for her morning tea after all.

She handed the bottle back to him with a "thank you."

He took it with a smile and brought it to his own lips. The prudent thing to do would have been to look away, but she stared as he took a long drink, his Adam's apple bobbing up and down as he swallowed. There was something very intimate about his mouth being on the same surface hers had just been on.

With a quiet squeak of embarrassment, Mel turned around and faced the water pump instead of Jaylen. She refused to look at him as he came and stood next to her.

"I'll need some supplies," he said. "But I think I can fix it."

It took a minute for his words to sink in, but when they did, Mel let out a squeal. "You can?" She clapped her hands like a little kid. "Thank you so much!"

On instinct, she flung herself at Jaylen. He was a touch too tall for her to reach over his shoulders comfortably, so she wrapped her arms around his midsection, pinning his arms to his sides. As soon as her cheek pressed against his body, she realized how inappropriate she was being and quickly stepped away.

She cleared her throat, which felt bone dry. "Sorry."

"No worries." He smiled at her indulgently. It was the kind of smile Mel might've given a student who was telling a drawn-out story that made little sense to her but was of utmost importance to them. "Is there a hardware store around here?"

"It's a couple of towns over, but we can bike there." She noticed how late it had gotten, the sun well behind the trees and the sky turning a pre-twilight periwinkle. "We can go tomorrow morning."

"Sounds good." Jaylen gathered up his belongings, slinging the many straps over his shoulders. "See you tomorrow morning."

He headed off toward the cabin, presumably back to the road and wherever he planned on staying the night.

"Wait!" she called.

He turned around but was shrouded in shadows so she couldn't read his expression. She went and caught up with him.

"I can make you dinner," she offered. That self-conscious feeling crept up on her again. "If you'd like…no pressure."

"Like your water pump." He let out a chuckle, but Mel stared at him in confusion. "Because your water pump has no pressure. Never mind. Stupid joke."

"Oh." Her eyes widened in understanding. "I get it. Very punny."

And with that, it was her turn to be embarrassed. But Jaylen genuinely laughed at her own stupid joke.

She swatted his arm. "Don't. That was so bad."

"No worse than mine." He took a deep breath as if stealing himself to give her bad news, but all he said was "dinner sounds nice."

"Okay." She smiled. Tonight, she had a dinner companion. It was a dream she never dared dream because it was so unbelievable.

They walked to the cabin side-by-side, and Mel found her dark thoughts from earlier grew farther away with each step.

CHAPTER 7

Mel stopped short of inviting Jaylen into the cabin. That was her space and her space alone. She left him with a promise to meet on the porch in an hour.

Where Jaylen went in the meantime was his own business. Perhaps back to where he came from—wherever that was! Mel hadn't ruled out the possibility that he had spawned from a magical mushroom.

The question that remained was what to make for dinner? Even though the weather had started to warm, fresh food was not in full supply yet. Mel's new crops had only begun to grow or were still being planted. Bounty time was summer and fall, not spring.

That didn't mean Mel was reluctant to offer Jaylen a meal. Far from it, she was eager to share one with him—with anyone other than the crows and chickens. No offense to her beloved birds, but they weren't much for conversation. Unfortunately, that self-conscious feeling crept up on her again, this time over what she could offer Jaylen.

Mel surveyed the small kitchen area. It consisted of a sink with a window above it that afforded a view to the front porch of the cabin. A small counter and a set of upper and lower cabinets flanked the sink. Drying herbs hung from the bottom of the upper cabinets, waiting to be bundled and stored. Potted plants took up most of the counter space with one small area kept open for food prep.

A small, round table with two chairs filled the middle of the room. Along the back wall of the cabin stood the wood burning stove with a built-in oven and stovetop. Next to that was a couch that separated the kitchen/living area from what Mel referred to as the bedroom. This part of the cabin consisted of a queen-sized bed, a bookshelf, and a window. The stove was the only source of heat in the house, so it made sense that it was all essentially one room.

There were two exceptions to this. The first was the bathroom, the only room in the house with its own door. It was to the right of the bedroom area and consisted of a composting toilet, a tiny sink, and a stall shower. The bathroom had running water—when the pump was working —but it wasn't heated. Cold showers were tolerable in the warmer months, but Mel usually heated up a bucket of water on the stove and used that for bathing in the winter.

The second area was on the left side near the front door, which was offset rather than centered along the front of the cabin. A wall with an open doorway separated it from the big room. Originally, it was for storing skiing and snowboarding equipment. Mel had converted it into a pantry by installing extra shelving all along the walls.

It didn't take her long to comb through the whole cabin and find her options somewhat lacking. There was the fresh cornbread from this morning. Well, the version of cornbread she could make without many of the traditional ingredients. A lack of leaveners made all her breads quite literally fall flat. She did her best with whipped egg whites, but it didn't always yield that fluffy bread consistency Mel once loved.

Cornbread was a start, but that wouldn't be enough, especially for someone of Jaylen's stature. Surely he needed more calories in a meal than Mel was used to consuming.

The pantry produced pickled green beans and dried apples with cinnamon, the latter of which she usually ate as a dessert. Her stores of cinnamon were slightly past their "best by" date, but she wasn't worried about that. She was pretty sure her grandmother had only ever used the same big tin of cinnamon throughout Mel's whole childhood and it never went bad.

A fresh basket of eggs sat on one of the shelves as well. With her trusty chickens, Mel had all the eggs she could ever want, but she wasn't in the mood for eggs.

She had a particular green thumb for lettuces and herbs and had success growing them in pots indoors, so that was a year-round staple. But there wasn't anything terribly interesting about a pile of romaine and arugula when there was nothing to dress it with besides pickling juice. When she realized she didn't have water to wash the greens, she disregarded the idea of salad altogether.

The cornbread, pickled vegetables, and apples would have to be enough for tonight. She pulled out two plates—what a novelty it was to use more than one plate for a meal—and set up the food on them, giving Jaylen a larger portion of everything.

From an outsider's perspective, it looked meager, but she shushed that thought away. Jaylen didn't seem the type to scoff at her food offerings. And if he did, he could go find his own dinner!

It was with a quiet thanks that she could provide a meal for two that she opened the front door to find Jaylen patiently waiting for her on the porch in one of the rocking chairs. The whole other side of the porch was filled with plants, mostly herbs and greens, and stacked wood. That way she didn't have to trek too far to keep the wood stove going.

It was growing cold and dark as the night settled in, so Mel went back inside to grab a warm sweater and some candles to set out along the wooden porch railing.

Jaylen and Mel sat side-by-side in the rocking chairs, carefully balancing the plates in their laps. He took a bite of cornbread and nodded appreciatively. They settled into a companionable silence as they ate, Mel stealing glances at Jaylen.

When a light breeze kissed the small flames of the candles, it sent the light dancing across his features, adding mystery to this man. He glanced at Mel as if about to ask a question and caught her staring. She quickly looked down at her plate, speared a pickled green bean with her fork, and shoved it into her mouth.

A glance out of the corner of her eyes proved Jaylen's attention had returned to his food. Mel breathed a sigh of relief and went back to eating.

Night noises rose up around them, the chirps and peeps of the forest in early spring and the sporadic hoot of an owl. Mel was careful not to get caught staring again, though she did sneak a peek now and then at him. She wondered if he was doing the same thing, only with more skill than she had because she didn't once catch him staring.

Finally as the plates grew empty, she broke the silence. "I'm sorry I didn't offer you a drink. I usually have water with dinner and only keep a small supply stored away. With the pump down, I figure I better save what I have for now."

She had suddenly remembered the supply of wine stowed away in her pantry. She only ever used it for cooking, but she wasn't opposed to sharing a glass with Jaylen. "I have wine. I could open a bottle.”

“No, thank you,” he said. “This is perfect like this. Best meal I’ve had in ages.”

A heat rose in Mel’s cheeks. “Well, in that case, would you like more?”

“No, you’ve been more than hospitable. Can I help clean up?”

She took her plate off her lap and stood. “No, thank you! I’ll take care of it.” She wasn’t ready to invite him into the cabin.

He also stood. The heat level in her body rose even more as he handed her his plate, their hands brushing slightly in the transfer.

“In that case,” he dipped his head politely at her, a grin pulling at his lips, “have a good night, ma’am.”

She laughed at his jest. Emotion welled up inside her and a lump formed in her throat. She cleared her throat, yet her voice was still husky when she said, “You too.”

Hands full with the two plates, Mel let her gaze linger over Jaylen’s form as he walked down the porch steps into the night.

The next morning, Mel woke with the sun as usual. She stoked the wood burning stove and retrieved the tea kettle. It wasn't until she tried to fill it with water and found the tap dry that she recalled what had happened the day before. She wasn't alone in the world anymore!

Her hand flew to her mouth with the shock of remembering. She blamed her bleary morning brain for the lapse in memory. How could she have forgotten Jaylen?

With cheeks blazing at the thought of the way the sun had haloed his hair the first time she'd seen him, she patted her messy hair and wondered if it was worth trying to tame the frizzy curls. Then, she silently chastised herself for worrying about what he would think of her hair of all things. She was acting like a girl with a school crush.

It wasn't a crush. It was simply an amiable reaction to connecting with another human being for the first time in years. Her slightly elevated heart rate and sweaty palms were normal in light of the situation.

She distracted herself by heading to the pantry to find the glass jars where she kept backup water. She put just enough in the kettle for one cup of tea and set it on the stove to boil. She tried not to think of Jaylen while she filled the strainer with a mix of herbs. There would be an abundance of fresh herbs soon enough, but today she would settle for dried ones: a lot of lemon balm and a touch of lavender to ease her mind.

Who was she kidding? There was no getting that man out of her thoughts. Her cheeks remained warm as she readied herself while she waited for the water to be ready.

The cabin was cold in the corners where the heat from the stove didn't reach particularly well, indicating it was cold outside. Despite the momentary heat of her body, she dressed warmly in her nicest pair of jeans, a sweater, and thick socks. She covered her hair in a knit hat, not because she might run into Jaylen but because it was cold outside.

At least, that's what she told herself as she took the strainer out of her tea and stirred thoughtfully.

Warm mug in hands, she headed outside to the coop and fed the hens and Gilbert. Rachel Lynde waddled over first, as usual. Mel made sure everyone got some cornbread before heading to the big pine tree upon which the crows liked to perch.

She didn't see them, so she clicked her tongue to alert them of her presence and scattered cornbread pieces on the ground. Disappointment settled over her as none of the crows came to greet her. Maybe they were busy.

Years ago, she and Daniel had hauled a set of wooden Adirondack chairs up to the yard. She settled into one of the chairs, not dwelling over the fact that one was always going to be empty. She sat quietly eating her cornbread and sipping her tea while waiting to see if the birds would come.

Instead, a different visitor showed up that made Mel forget all about being stood up by the crows. Jaylen approached from the road, his boots heavy on the dirt driveway. He was wearing a puffy coat and rubbing his hands together as he strode toward her with a confident gait.

Mel wondered where he'd slept and if he'd stayed warm overnight. Maybe she should have made him tea, though he didn't come off as a tea drinker. Then again, who could afford to be picky about morning beverages these days?

"Chilly this morning." He flashed her a smile, one she found she could get used to.

"Mmmm," she agreed, wishing she was more immune to this man's charms.

She sipped her tea to avoid having to figure out what to say that wouldn't be awkward or an overshare. The art of small talk was one she had never been particularly good at, given she had spent a good deal of her adult life with five-year-olds. Now, she was sure she'd be even worse at it with being so out of practice.

"Is that coffee?" Jaylen asked with raised eyebrows.

"Tea. My own home brew. Would you like me to make you a cup?" She tried not to be disappointed when his hopeful expression faded away. She had correctly guessed he was not a tea drinker.

"No, thanks." He tucked his hands into his coat pockets and blew out a breath. "Man, I miss coffee. The smell of a fresh pot. That first too-hot sip. Nothing quite like it to wake you up in the morning."

"Mmmm," she said again and took another sip, proving she was, in fact, very bad at this whole conversing thing. She blurted out, "I miss cheese."

"Cheese?" There was that smile again from him. "What's your favorite kind?"

"A good sharp New York cheddar." It seemed like a simple choice, but cheddar cheese was so versatile. Eat a slice by itself, put it on a cracker, add a pepperoni slice, grill it in between thick slices of bread.

"Oh, yes. Cheddar's the best for homemade mac n' cheese." He smacked his lips together. "You're stirring up all kinds of cravings in me this morning."

A tingling sensation crept up Mel's neck, and she found herself quite speechless thinking about what he was craving. Why was she so awkward around this man?

Jaylen glanced around as if looking for something else to talk about, and his gaze fell on the cornbread at the base of the pine tree. "Do you let the chickens out of the coop to eat?"

"Oh, no. It was hard enough to get them in there in the first place. Rachel Lynde nearly pecked my eye out."

"Rachel Lynde?" Jaylen asked.

"The gray one—that's her name. After the character in the *Anne of Green Gables* series." She rambled off the names of all the other hens, finishing with "Gilbert is the rooster."

"I see." His grin was wide as he gestured at the food on the ground. "So who is that for?"

"The crows. They're really smart. They usually come around in the morning, and I share breakfast with them."

"Do the crows have names?"

"No...well, just the one. Tiny Tim." Mel hid her face in her cup. Her armpits grew warm under her sweater. Avoiding looking directly at him, she sought a change in subject. "Do you want breakfast?"

"No, thank you. I already ate. I was thinking we could head out to the hardware store soon."

Mel slid out of the Adirondack chair in the most dignified way she could manage, which was not very dignified at all. She would never understand the design of those chairs. But at least she didn't fall flat on her face.

"Let me get ready. Then we can bike there."

"Yes, ma'am."

She heard the tease in his voice but was far too embarrassed to find any pleasure in the jest. "I'll meet you out front in a few."

He nodded as she headed back to the cabin. She was determined to stay focused on the task at hand, which was getting the materials to fix the water pump. She would not let Jaylen drive her to distraction again.

CHAPTER 9

Not only was Mel determined not to be distracted by Jaylen, she was resolute in not being self-conscious around him. Even with all the challenges of this world, she liked her life. Some might have called it simple—if there had been others around to observe it—but it was as rich as she could make it. There was no reason to feel bad about who she was or to pretend that she was someone she wasn't.

So many new feelings were stirring up inside her as she made sure her clothing was layered properly. This morning was chilly, but the day would warm and she would be prepared for it, as she always was.

Though, there had been no preparing for Jaylen. But, really, who could have expected another person to show up when it seemed everyone else in the world was dead?

She hadn't been ready for him yesterday, but she would be ready for him now. And that meant being her true self no matter what. If he judged her for it, that was his problem.

Mel left the hat on her bed, not that she could wear it with her bike helmet, and fluffed out her hair with her hands. Then, she packed a small lunch and a canteen of water and met Jaylen on the porch.

He was sitting in the same chair where he'd had dinner last night, leaning back into it as if he were perfectly comfortable. As if he owned the chair. As if he'd done it a million times, instead of just the once.

Instead of feeling presumptuous, it came off as comfortable.

Jaylen was an easy-going guy, Mel realized. Not like her late husband. Daniel had been passionate and, to be honest, a bit high-strung. He had felt things strongly and wasn't afraid to share that. There was comfort in always knowing where she stood with Daniel, but the man himself wouldn't have been described as easy-going.

She shook her head of thoughts of her husband and looked to Jaylen. "Ready?"

"Yes, ma'am."

She groaned inwardly. How long before she put a stop to the whole "ma'am" thing?

"We can take the bikes," she said as she led him to the shed. "But I don't think I have a helmet that will fit you."

"That's okay. I'll take my chances without one." Jaylen gestured to the overgrown driveway where the truck stood. "Does your truck still run?"

"Not in years."

Jaylen stared thoughtfully at it, and Mel might have said he looked like he was getting ideas about what he could do with the truck. But she didn't know him well enough to be sure.

She pulled open the doors to the shed and went in to retrieve the bikes. It was an old wooden shed, having been here before Mel and Daniel bought the property, but sturdy and without leaks.

There were no windows and it sat in a shady area near

the tree line, so it was dark when with just the light from the open doors. Jaylen stepped in behind her, and she waited a minute to let her eyes adjust.

She pointed at the olive green bike. "You can take that one."

As Mel went to lift the kickstand to her yellow bike, Jaylen let out a hearty laugh.

She looked around and wondered what could possibly be so hilarious about an old shed. "What's so funny?"

Her earlier resolve at not being self-conscious diminished as each moment passed and Jaylen continued to laugh.

"Sorry." He wiped tears from his eyes. "I'm not making fun."

"Huh," Mel huffed. It sure felt like he was.

"It's just..." Jaylen rubbed at his beard. "It's like a warehouse in here. You sure are prepared."

Scanning the shed with a new perspective in mind, Mel took in the supplies she had acquired. There were the bikes and plenty of gardening tools, like planters, watering cans, shovels, a hoe, and a manual lawn mower. Near those were an axe and a couple different kinds of hand saws. All normal stuff for a shed.

Then there were the metal shelves that housed candles, boxes of matches, yellow no. 2 pencils, a stack of notebooks, and bars of soap taken in bulk from the wholesale store, among other things. She was lucky the mature trees next to the shed kept it shaded most of the day, so she didn't have to worry about the candles or soap melting.

With a pang, she was reminded of her classroom closet of fresh supplies at the beginning of each year. The musty scent of the shed was replaced with that of lemon cleaner and the hint of melted plastic from the laminated name labels on each desk. That was the smell of a new school year.

Mel swallowed back tears at that memory.

Jaylen's reaction to the supplies in the shed made her very happy she hadn't invited him inside the cabin. What if he had looked under the bed and seen the t-shirts, underwear, and socks she stored there, all sealed in their plastic packaging? Or if he had gone into the cabinet in her bathroom and seen the medicine and toiletries she horded there? They were all expired now, but expired toothpaste did the job just fine and the medicine was for emergencies.

All of this had been gathered after her trip on the one-year anniversary of Daniel's death when Mel had vowed to live her life in the way she wanted. No more canned food. No more wallowing in sorrow.

That when she started her garden here at the cabin, and it wasn't long before she could sustain herself with the food she grew and foraged, the eggs from her chickens, and the occasional fishing trip. Mel wasn't a fan of fish—either the preparation or the taste—but it was a good source of nutrition.

She had calculated the type and amount of supplies she would need to make it to 100 years old. An optimistic estimate to be sure, but better to overestimate such things rather than run short. Hence all the stuff in the cabin and shed. She would be prepared for whatever this solitary life could throw at her, and she'd do her best to find moments of joy.

Jaylen stood very still next to her. He wasn't laughing anymore.

As if to prove how useful the supplies were, she grabbed a few candles and a box of matches and shoved them in her backpack. "I've done what I had to do."

"Of course." His voice was a deep timbre, more solemn

than she had yet to hear it. "We all have. I admire you in your preparedness."

She felt him looking at her, but she kept her gaze on the bike handlebars she gripped beneath trembling hands.

"You're not what I was expecting," he admitted.

"Well," Mel said with an attempt at a breezy voice. "I wasn't expecting you at all."

She wheeled the bike out of the shed. The sudden brightness outside had tears welling in her eyes. His words about Mel not being what he expected stuck with her, but she wasn't going to let it bother her.

She took the helmet from where it hung from the handlebars and placed it on her head, unceremoniously smashing down her unruly hair. She pushed the bike forward along the dirt driveway and gestured for Jaylen to come along without looking back at him.

At the entrance to the road, Mel mounted the bike and headed off down the hill. The breeze on her cheeks calmed her, as it always did. Clouds had gathered overhead, so there was no strip of sunshine in the middle of the road to warm her. No matter, she would enjoy this bike ride despite the lack of sunshine, and despite the lack of sensitivity of this man who had barged into her life so abruptly.

He was going fix her water pump, so she would tolerate him. She needn't care what he thought of her or her supplies. He was a means to an end. That was all.

Chapter 10

While the library was in the town closest to Mel's cabin, the hardware store was a couple of towns over. It was a good thing they had set out in the morning because it would probably take most of the daylight hours to bike there, find what they needed, and get back.

That was if the store had what Jaylen needed to fix the water pump. He hadn't specifically said what that was, but she trusted he knew what he was doing. He was an aerospace engineer after all.

She cruised along, the weather not warming as she had expected but staying cool with the cloud cover and an occasional gusty wind. The mostly downhill ride required more braking than pedaling, and they made good time. A few glances back showed that Jaylen was there but keeping his space. Perhaps in deference for laughing at her or more likely because he didn't know the way to the hardware store.

At the end of the winding road where the Thirsty Crow Tavern stood, instead of her usual right to the library, Mel took a left. The hum of Jaylen's bike followed in her wake. With the road leveling out, she kept their pace steady but not overtaxing.

This ride was longer than the one to the library but shorter than other rides she did seasonally. She visited a pick-your-own farm a few times a year for strawberries in late spring, blueberries in summer, and apples in the fall. She loved stocking up on fresh fruit. She would eat her fill while they were fresh. The apples were her favorite because they stayed fresh for weeks after picking.

For a year-round treat, she made jam with the strawberries and blueberries and dried the apples. The apples were also important because she could make apple cider vinegar with them, which served as pickling juice for the vegetables she grew. She had learned so much about how to preserve food without refrigeration that she often forgot all the measures she took to stay fed in winter.

The wind picked up as they approached the hardware store, and Mel shivered. To her dismay, the clouds had thickened with the threatening look of a rainstorm. The weather had seemed promising this morning, but with no weather forecast to rely on, Mel was always taking a chance with a trip away from the cabin. She pumped her legs faster to pick up the pace.

Pretty soon, she pulled into the parking lot of the hardware store, Jaylen turning in behind her. The building was larger and more modern-looking than many of the establishments in the small mountain towns in the area. Mel had taken many trips here when she and Daniel had first bought the cabin. The kitchen cabinets and sink had come from here, among other smaller items.

The last time she had been here was about a month ago to get a wood post to repair a section of the chicken coop. She never did figured out how that particular post had snapped. The chickens certainly weren't big enough to have done it.

She might have suspected a larger animal, but there were none left in the area as far as Mel knew. That meant the only predators left in the mountains were hawks. They could certainly eat the chickens, but they weren't likely to break a post. Perhaps a rogue reptile had found its way to Mel's yard. She shuddered thinking of an alligator making its way up to New York from Florida.

And now her imagination was running wild!

She cleared away the thoughts and parked her bike under the store's entryway, taking off her helmet and leaving it hanging from the handlebars. Jaylen parked next to her. She had long ago broken the glass of the sliding door that no longer worked without electricity, so she slipped through the opening without a word. Jaylen dutifully came in after her.

From her bag, Mel took out the box of matches, a candle, and a candle holder. She'd learned long ago that the drippings from a candle were hot enough to burn skin. She stuck the candle in the holder, swiped a match, and lit up the candle. The entrance was graced with light coming in from the front doors, but a little farther in proved much darker. The candlelight barely reached past their immediate area.

"Where are the electrical supplies?" Jaylen asked in a quiet voice that nonetheless echoed eerily in the abandoned store.

Ask her where the electrical books were in the library, and she'd be able to point you in the right spot in the nonfiction section. But departments in the hardware store? That wasn't her forte. She remembered the garden section was to the right. A closer look with the candle at the aisle straight ahead revealed the paint section.

Mel pointed to the left. "Maybe that way. Sorry, I've never needed electrical supplies."

Why would she need them when she hadn't had

electricity since moving up to the cabin?

She handed him the candle. She was no help to him beyond this point, so he might as well lead. Jaylen stared at her for a beat longer than necessary but eventually headed to the left.

He peered down each aisle as they passed until he found one of interest and headed down it. Mel followed slightly behind. She could have lit the second candle and gone off on her own, but she had no desire to do that. Being here made her feel uneasy.

It wasn't that she was afraid she'd get lost and not be able to find him again, no that wasn't it. Something about the size of the place unnerved her.

She didn't like the way the candlelight didn't even come close to reaching the ceiling. The library's ceiling was probably just as high, but with the large stain-glassed windows, it was always fairly bright in there during the day. This place was bigger, but without any natural light reaching most of the aisles, she somehow felt boxed in.

Jaylen stopped at a shelf and brought the candle closer to inspect the contents of it, stealing away some of the precious light. Mel leaned against the shelves opposite to where Jaylen was looking, the solidness of them behind her comforting.

That was until a shuffling noise came from right behind her. She turned slowly and backed away. The shuffling noises grew louder.

A small shadowy figure burst from the shelf, straight toward Mel's face. She screamed.

CHAPTER 11

As the shadow darted toward Mel, she backed up until she ran smack into something warm and firm. A hand slipped around her waist, gripping her firmly in place. The area next to her was suddenly awash with light.

It was Jaylen with the candle, of course. Who else would it have been?

The candlelight illuminated the shadow, which proved to be nothing more than a small songbird fluttering about. Mel had probably frightened it as much as it had frightened her.

The bird continued its confused flight for a moment before rising high enough to be out of the light's reach. Mel stood perfectly still with Jaylen at her back, his arm tight around her, while she listened to the beat of the bird's wings until they quieted. Presumably, the bird had landed somewhere nearby.

"Are you okay?" Jaylen's deep voice this close to her ear startled her, but his firm grip kept her in place.

His question echoed the first words he had ever spoken to her. They were as sincere now as they had been then, but this time, the words—and his touch—held an intimacy that hadn't been there before.

"I'm alright," she breathed.

She allowed herself a minute for her nerves to settle, the only sounds her ragged breaths and Jaylen's quiet ones close to her ear. Then, she slipped out of his embrace, the air cold against her back as she lost the warmth of Jaylen's body.

He angled the candle toward the shelf where the bird had come from. Behind a selection of metal electrical boxes the light revealed a bird's nest with two small eggs inside.

"Oh," Mel said. "Poor mama bird."

"Let's get what we need and then we can leave her in peace." He moved a little farther down the aisle and continued to search for what he needed.

Mel scooted away from the nest, closer to Jaylen. "I hope she comes back to the nest."

"I'm sure she will."

While Jaylen shuffled through a bunch of hanging items Mel couldn't tell the difference between, she thought about the eggs and hoped the mama bird wouldn't abandon them.

She and Daniel had never had children of their own. Ten years ago, she'd been diagnosed with adenomyosis and eventually had a hysterectomy. She had been a little sad to get the final word that she would never bear children, but she had her class of twenty or so new children to nurture every year. That had been enough.

Now that she thought about it, she supposed the hysterectomy had been a blessing in disguise. The pain of losing every single one of her students had been bad enough. And Daniel's death had felt unbearable; she had barely made it through that. She probably would have given up entirely if she had lost a child of her own, too.

Mel was lost in her thoughts when Jaylen snatched an

item off the hooks and handed it to her. "Can you hold this for me?"

She stared at the merchandise without really seeing as she popped it into her backpack. Lingering on the past was not a good idea. She forced her mind into the present, focusing on Jaylen as he perused through the shelves.

He selected more items, handing each one over for Mel to stash in her backpack.

He paused, his thumb touching the tips of his fingers in turn as if counting or taking stock of what he had gathered. Then, he muttered, "One more thing."

Slowly moving back along the aisle, the candle held aloft for a better view, Jaylen perused the shelves again.

"Ah, here it is." He handed Mel one more package. "That should do it. Let's leave mama bird alone, shall we?"

She zipped up her bag and nodded, letting him lead the way out of the store. She sent a silent little whisper to the mama bird that they were gone, hoping with all her heart that she would return to her eggs, as they walked through the broken front door.

Outside, a darkened sky and whipping wind greeted them. Mel stepped out from the cover of the awning at the store entrance and looked west. Even darker clouds graced the sky there. But there was no rain...yet.

"Do you think that storm is headed our way?" Jaylen asked.

Mel stared at the sky. The storm was in the opposite direction of the cabin, but based on the direction storms usually moved around there, it was headed toward them.

"Probably."

"Thought so. Do you think we'll make it back before it hits?"

With how quickly the clouds were churning and the

wind was gusting, she doubted they would be able to out-ride it.

"Probably not," she admitted.

"Do you want to stay here and wait it out?"

She looked back through the broken glass into the dark store. A strange sensation of unease had settled over her the moment they had entered, and it had only worsened with the bird encounter and the thoughts of children. Staying any longer did not appeal to her. Plus, she didn't want to risk disturbing the bird again.

Mel's life was one of calculation. The way she carefully counted out every seed she planted, how she organized and cataloged her food supply, the lifetime supply of underwear waiting for her under her bed. The smart thing—the safe thing—would be to stay.

But constant calculation and caution had grown tedious. Today, she would throw caution to the wind and try to outrun the storm, and maybe outrun her thoughts as well.

She shot Jaylen a devilish grin. "Let's ride."

"Okay."

He mounted his bike and waited as she hastily put on her helmet, flipped up the kickstand, and got on her bike.

"Follow me!" she shouted.

Jaylen whooped as they pedaled out of the parking lot into the street, a couple of fat raindrops wetting the ground behind them.

Chapter 12

Mel pushed her strength and stamina to the limit as she tried to move faster than the storm, Jaylen barely keeping up with her. But no matter how fast they pumped the pedals, the rain chased them. And it was about to win.

The raindrops arrived sporadically at first, but before long, they began to come down in earnest. The sky darkened more than Mel thought possible in the daytime, making visibility very low. Then, the downpour arrived, drenching them in seconds and turning the road into a river.

They were on flat terrain for now, not having reached the turnoff at the Thirsty Crow yet, but it would be all uphill after that.

A gust of wind sent the rain sideways. Mel squinted to try and keep the water out of her eyes, but it was a losing battle. She risked taking one hand off the steering wheel to swipe her face clean. A mistake.

The bike veered to the right. She quickly gripped the handlebars with both hands again, but it was too late.

She hadn't realized how close she was to the side of the road until the front tire of the bike hit the spot where the road met grass. The change in terrain stopped the front tire immediately. The back end of the bike came around fast, pitching Mel off of it.

She landed on her side and slid across the wet grass before coming to a stop just shy of where the ground sloped down into a ditch. Rain pounded down, echoing in her head as it hit her helmet.

Mel lay perfectly still, except for the rapid rise and fall of her chest, and assessed her body. The right side of her torso where it had slid across the ground stung, but nothing seemed to be broken. She groaned and sat up.

Jaylen skidded his bike to a stop near where hers had fallen. He ran over and flopped down on his knees next to her. His hands kind of fluttered around her body as if he wanted to check for injuries but was afraid to touch her.

His mouth moved, but Mel couldn't hear what he was saying. The storm was so loud. She blinked against the rain, too winded to ask him to repeat himself. Without a helmet, water sluiced down Jaylen's face worse than hers, leaving shiny streaks along his dark skin.

"Are you okay?" Jaylen shouted, and Mel heard him this time.

It was the second time today he had asked that. It was an indication of how off-track her life had gotten that he seemed to always be questioning if she was okay.

She managed a nod as shivers began to wrack her body.

He stood and held out a hand. "Can you stand?"

Mel finally found her voice. "I think so."

She took his hand and he gently helped her up. Her right ankle gave out as she tried to put weight on it. Jaylen caught her before she fell back down into the grass, his arms wrapping around her. She sucked in a breath when his hand touched the side she had fallen on.

"Sorry!" he yelled. "What hurts?"

"My ankle, and my side." Her teeth chattered in between words as she pointed toward the right side of her body.

He didn't let go, merely shifted his support away from her injuries, kind of huddling around her from the side. She leaned her left side up against his body, putting a lot of her weight on him. Now that she had noticed the pain, her ankle was hurting very badly.

His upper body tilted over her in a kind of cocoon that blocked out some of the rain. He really was very tall. The steady rise and fall of his chest against her was a small comfort.

Jaylen paused and looked around...for what, she wasn't sure.

"We need to get out of this rain," he said.

The rain was falling as hard as ever. They were both thoroughly soaked. Mel's gaze darted around as she tried to gather her bearings. She couldn't see very far down the road, but she recognized this stretch.

"The library," she said. "It's not far from here."

"Can you walk?" Jaylen gazed down at her with concern in his big brown eyes.

Mel gingerly set her ankle on the slick ground and tested it. She hissed when a sharp pain radiated up her leg.

"I don't think so."

"Can you stand for a sec?"

"Yes." She hoped she could do that at least.

Jaylen slowly pulled away from her, staying close until she proved she could keep herself upright on her own. She kept most of the weight on her left foot with just enough on her right to keep her balance. The pain had numbed a bit, perhaps from the cold. She shivered when the wind gusted and hoped it wouldn't knock her over.

He ran over to his bike and propped it up with the kickstand before hurrying back to her. "Ready?"

"Ready for what?"

"I'll carry you over to the bike. You sit on it, and I'll push it to the library."

The thought of getting back on a bike was unappealing to put it mildly. But it was probably the best option as she wasn't confident she could walk anywhere right now.

"Okay," she relented.

Jaylen scooped her up in his arms, backpack and all, and carried her to the bike. He was so gentle in his movements that her sore side barely hurt. She helped him guide her onto the seat and reached out to grip the handlebars. She wasn't sure what to do with her feet. Putting them on the petals would be more movement than her ankle could handle once they started going. She kind of criss-crossed them on the frame, careful to give her hurting ankle the support it needed.

With Jaylen standing next to the bike, his sturdy arms reaching around either side of her, he placed his hands next to hers on the handlebars.

"Ready?" he asked her again.

This time she was ready. She nodded and pointed in the direction of the library.

The bike was a little unsteady at first as Jaylen got the hang of moving forward while keeping his legs clear of the pedals. Then they were off toward the library. Rain pelting down on them with every step.

Chapter 13

Mel was shivering uncontrollably by the time they reached the library. The adrenaline of the crash was wearing off, and she was just sitting there on the bike, barely moving. The cold spring rain felt like it was seeping into her bones.

She directed Jaylen to the side door of the old Roman Gothic building. He wheeled the bike right inside with her on it, bumping over the threshold as comfortably as he could. He helped her off the bike, but she waved off his efforts to carry her.

A cold numbness was setting in, muting the pain of Mel's injuries. This allowed her to hobble over with little assistance to the nearest sitting area. She untangled herself from her backpack and dropped it to the floor.

With a groan at the effort, she sat. It was several moments before she bothered to take off the helmet and set it next to the backpack. A dripping wet Jaylen hovered over her, but she paid him little mind.

She was too cold to focus on anything in particular. The rain had soaked through every layer of her clothing and quickly began seeping into the upholstery of the chair. She wrapped her arms around herself as the shivers intensified.

The library, which usually felt so welcoming and full of possibilities, was cold and dark. The rain lashed the roof with an ominous pounding. The heavy cloud cover outside made it so not even the stained-glass windows could cheer up the place.

"Do you mind if I take a candle to look around?" Jaylen asked.

Mel shrugged noncommittally. He retrieved a candle and holder from her bag, lit the wick, and headed toward a door that led to an office area with desks and storage. She'd poked around in there a few times but never found anything of particular interest.

Alone now, Mel took the opportunity to lift her sweater and the layers underneath to inspect the side she had fallen on. The wet material stuck to her skin and smarted when she peeled it up. She sucked in a breath as she examined the damage.

No deep cuts, but a large area of grass burn had turned the skin red and raw. A purple bruise had already started to blossom above her hip. Something about seeing the wound refreshed the sting of it. The pain throbbed along with her pulse.

"That's going to need cleaning." Jaylen's voice startled her, and she quickly covered up her skin.

"It'll have to wait until we get home." She shifted in the chair, everything about this moment feeling uncomfortable.

Jaylen blew out the candle and set it on the floor. Then, he held out a pile of garments that had been tucked under his arm.

"Found some dry clothes."

Upon further inspection, most of the clothes turned out to be cardigans with an odd assortment of other items.

"I guess the stereotype about librarians and cardigans is true." Mel laughed despite how cold and awful she felt. "Elementary teachers, too. There were always a few cardigans lying around the teachers' room."

"You're a teacher?" Jaylen asked.

"I was." Past tense, as was the case with so many things that were once in the present tense. So many people, too.

"What grade?"

She picked at a loose button on a beige cardigan decorated with little owls. "Kindergarten."

Jaylen gave a "hmm" of acknowledgment but didn't push for more, seemingly sensing her reluctance to talk about her old job.

Mel held up a purple sequined jacket fit for a magician. "Where did you find this?"

"In a bin labeled 'costumes.'" He grinned. "I left the feather boas and tiaras behind, but I can get them if you want."

She laughed at the picture in her head of Jaylen wrapped in a boa, a shiny tiara perched on his head. "You know what? You should."

"Really?" His face lit up with mischief. "I will." He bounded off to where the offices were, not bothering to take the candle with him this time.

It gave Mel another moment of privacy to gather herself. Thinking about her colleagues, many of who had become friends over the years, and all her little students, threatened to put her in a bad head space.

She shook the memories away and picked through the clothes to find something suitable to change into. She settled on a set of black leggings and a long-sleeve shirt made of a similar material, along with the owl cardigan to layer over it. She wasn't shivering anymore, but she hadn't fully shaken the chill. Dry clothes would hopefully help with that if she could find a private space to change into them.

Mel held her foot up and gingerly rolled the ankle she had twisted. The pain was less than before and the range of motion was okay. She tested it out by standing on her good leg and carefully adding a little pressure to the injured one. She was able to limp to an aisle that concealed her enough to feel comfortable changing.

The clothes were musty smelling but dry and a whole lot warmer than what she had been wearing. She bundled the wet stuff into a ball and held it away from her so they didn't drip on her as she hobbled back to the chair.

Jaylen was back, having changed into dry clothes that included the sequined jacket. He was sitting on the floor, rifling through the bin of costumes. The chair was too wet to sit in, so Mel carefully lowered herself next to him.

He unearthed a feather boa and wrapped it around his neck. The boa was purple but somehow a different enough shade from the sequined jacket to clash with it. He completed the look with a flower crown, light blue ribbons cascading off the sides, framing his face. It was better than Mel had imagined!

"I saved this one for you." He held out a rainbow-patterned boa.

When he gently draped it over her shoulders, she felt the heat of him near her and shivered. Mistaking it for a chill, he asked, "Do you need another sweater?"

She cleared her throat. "No, I'm fine." He was still pretty close to her, so she batted at one of the ribbons hanging from the flower crown. "I like this."

He flashed her a smile and posed with his hands cupped under his bearded chin, his one dimple winking at her. The whole thing was so ridiculous that she burst into laughter.

Jaylen let out his own deep rumble.

Mel laughed so long and hard, she started to cough, and that sent her chaffed side hurting worse than ever. She winced, but couldn't stop laughing.

"Sorry, sorry," he apologized.

"It's okay," she managed to say, her laughter finally subsiding. And it was the truth. Things were okay in this moment, here in the library with Jaylen.

CHAPTER 14

While Jaylen hung up their wet clothes along the metal railing of the stairs to the catwalk, Mel took out the food she had brought for lunch. It was well past lunchtime now, and her stomach grumbled with hunger. All her meals were simple, and she was used to eating the same thing for days at a time, but this meal was simpler than usual.

Donning their silly outfits, they enjoyed the cornbread with blueberry jam and a side of roasted sunflower seeds. Normally, Mel would've packed hardboiled eggs, but she hadn't wanted to use her water reserves to make them this morning. The cornbread was a little smashed up after having been in the backpack during the bike crash, but it tasted good all the same.

She took a sip of water from the canteen and was about to offer it to Jaylen when she caught him licking the last of the blueberry jam off his thumb.

"Water?" she squeaked, knowing exactly why her voice came out that way.

He flashed her a smile, which did absolutely nothing to help with the butterflies flitting in her stomach.

"Thanks." He took a sip and wiped his lips with his sleeve, making a face when the ridiculous purple sequins touched his mouth. "Are you a vegetarian?"

"No," she answered, grateful for the distraction.

"Oh, cool. I wasn't sure because I know you eat eggs. I thought maybe you eat the chickens, too."

"I haven't eaten chicken since before."

She had considered it when Josie Pye had died, but without knowing the hen's cause of death, she couldn't be sure it was safe. Even if she had been able to eat the chicken safely, she wasn't sure she had the heart to eat what she considered to be a companion.

Instead, she had buried her in the woods and left a stick cross as a marker. Mel had never been particularly religious before the pandemic, and since then, well, she didn't have much use for religion these days. But the cross marker for Josie Pye had felt right in the moment.

"Okay, so no chicken," Jaylen said. "I haven't seen you eat any other kind of meat. Not that we've had many meals together. It would be presumptuous of me to think I know much about what you eat. But I also didn't want to presume you ate meat if you didn't."

Mel tried to suppress a smile. Maybe she wasn't the only one who had grown out of practice in the art of conversation. "I'll eat meat. It's just not something I'm comfortable procuring myself."

"Gotcha. Because I have goose jerky and was wondering if you'd like some."

"Goose jerky...like dried strips of goose meat?"

"Yes, ma'am."

Lip twitching at his use of "ma'am," she opened her mouth to decline, but he cut in, "I see your skepticism, but it's actually pretty tasty. And it's a good protein source."

Mel tried to school her face into a neutral expression as Jaylen produced a small metal container from his pocket and twisted off the top. He took a dark piece of leathery meat from it, popped it in his mouth, and began to chew. Then, he held the container out to her.

Hesitantly, she peered into the tin and selected the smallest piece she could find. She didn't have any experience eating wild game. She might have learned to hunt if there had been any mammals left after the pandemic, but she hadn't seen a wolf, rabbit, squirrel, or even a single field mouse in over five years.

The closest thing she did to hunting was the occasional fishing trip. There was a lake within hiking distance that had yellow perch, but it wasn't easy to transport fish back to the cabin. Usually, she'd build a fire lakeside and cook up the perch with some greens. If she caught enough she'd bring the leftovers home to make soup the next day. It was kind of a long trip that took up a lot of energy, so it wasn't something she did that often.

It had never occurred to her to eat goose. She wasn't a fan of the fish preparation. She always looked away when she had to peel the head and spine from the meat of the fish. She nearly gagged at the thought of preparing the goose with all those feathers.

Jaylen watched her sniff the jerky as he ate another piece. It gave off a slight peppery smell that wasn't unappealing. She contemplated taking a nibble to test it out, but one look at his expectant face had her shoving the whole piece in her mouth.

She chewed for what felt like a long time, all with Jaylen carefully observing her. Mel had never understood what people meant when they described food as gamy, but now she totally got it. There were hints of spices somewhere in there, but her sense of taste was completely overwhelmed by what could only be described as the utter gaminess of the goose.

"What do you think?" he asked as she finally stopped chewing and washed down the last bits of jerky with a sip of water.

"I'd say it's an acquired taste."

There was a glint in Jaylen's eyes as he asked, "You want more?"

"Maybe later," she said, glad she hadn't hurt his feelings over not caring for his offering.

"You don't hunt, do you?"

"I'm more of a grow your own food kind of person." It wasn't a direct answer, but it was answer enough.

She mentioned her fishing trips and wondered if Jaylen would stick around long enough to want to go on one with her. Maybe they could even camp out by the lake for a night. It wasn't something she would have wanted to do on her own, but it could be fun with another person, especially if that person were Jaylen.

"I'd love to learn more about the food you grow," he said.

"I'm happy to share what I know." And she was, both happy to share and happy to have him stick around long enough to learn.

"You seem to do all right for yourself, but if you ever wanted to learn how to hunt, I could teach you."

She recalled the rifle slung over his shoulder the day she met him. She hadn't seen it since then. The thought of a bullet piercing a goose's neck and the blood gushing had her swallowing back saliva.

"I'll keep that in mind" was all she said.

Jaylen stretched, saying he was going to check on the weather as he stood and headed outside. The heavy downpour had quieted during their meal, though various dripping sounds came from the roof.

Mel unwrapped her feet from the cardigan she had placed around them in place of her soaked socks. Her hurt ankle was swollen, and faint purple bruise was visible under the ankle bone. She suspected the bruising would get worse before it got better. But when she rolled her ankle in tentative circles, she found the pain bearable.

At least, she was dry and warm now, so that was an improvement.

Jaylen's offer of teaching her to hunt had gotten her wondering about how long he planned on being here. She had never asked him what had brought him to this area in the first place. She had assumed chance had brought him to the cabin to find her crashing out over the broken water pump.

But the more she thought about it, the more it seemed like a pretty big coincidence that he had found her at all. There was really nothing to attract him to this part of upstate New York these days. Had he simply been wandering? Had he been on the way to somewhere else?

More pressing, she supposed, was whether or not she cared why he was there and if he stayed. She decided not to think about it too hard because she wasn't sure she'd like the answer.

CHAPTER 15

Jaylen was gone longer than she expected, but he was a big boy so Mel wasn't worried. Even if she had wanted to see what he had gotten up to outside, her ankle was not feeling good enough to go out exploring. Restlessness crept up on her as she sat there waiting, so she decided to look for a new book. She was at a library after all!

Mel managed to stand up and bear her own weight with more of what she would call discomfort than pain. The rest of her body was also stiff, probably from sitting on the floor for so long.

There was a time when she went up and down on the floor all day with her kindergarten students. Apparently, her body had grown out of practice, or she was just getting old. Forty-five wasn't exactly ancient, but it wasn't young either. Then again, she had been thrown from her bike mere hours ago, so that could account for the stiffness. That's what she would go with—the fall, not old age.

Barefooted, she ventured to the nearest shelf and grabbed a random book. Even with the cloud cover, there was enough light coming into the library to read without lighting a candle. She settled down right there on the floor, her back up against the bookshelf.

The thriller book was out of her usual repertoire of genres. It was about a group of women taking a trip to a cabin in the woods for a "girls' vacation," only for things to go horribly wrong. Maybe not the best decision to pick an unsettling category while sitting in a darkening library, but she rarely had trouble losing herself in a good book. Soon, she was immersed deep in the forest with the five women, each of whom had a secret she didn't want the others to know.

"Hey, sorry I took so long." The voice came out of nowhere.

Mel shrieked and dropped the book on her uninjured foot. She hadn't heard Jaylen reenter the library, but there he was, standing at the end of the aisle, his shadow throwing her reading spot into pressing darkness. She held one trembling hand to her heart and used the other one to rub her big toe where the book had hit.

"Jaylen! You scared me."

"I can see that," he said, offering her a hand up. "Sorry. Good book?" He picked it up and glanced at the cover before handing it over.

"Yes." Mel looked around and noticed how dark the library had grown, even without Jaylen casting a shadow. "Though it's getting a bit dark to read. Where did you go?"

"To get your bike. The rain's mostly stopped, but the roads are wet and I don't think we'd make it back to your cabin before dark. We're stuck here for the night."

"Okay," she said with more resolve than she felt. This wasn't how she had expected the day to go when Jaylen had asked to go to the hardware store. She had hoped they'd get the parts for the pump and have her water back up and running before dark, but it was not to be. "It's probably best to rest my ankle anyway before attempting to bike up the hill."

"We can walk the bikes up the hill if we need to."

Mel shrugged. "We'll see tomorrow." The excitement of the day was catching up with her. She rolled her shoulders, which somehow elicited a huge yawn, and she almost lost her balance.

Jaylen shot her a concerned look as he steadied her. "Are you okay?"

"Yeah. Just tired and sore."

He hovered around her while she headed back to the chair. The upholstery was dry now, and she was relieved to be able to sit there instead of on the floor.

"How about I get things set up for the night?" Jaylen said.

She nodded and looked around, not sure what he meant by setting up. He retrieved the tin container from his pocket and handed her a piece of goose jerky, which she reluctantly took. They had eaten all the food she had packed, so it was all they had, and she could sure use the protein right now.

As she munched on the jerky, rotating bites of it with sips of water, Jaylen got to work. First, he lit the candles as night was rapidly creeping over the library. One he left on the floor near her chair. The other he took with him to the office. He left that one in there as he pulled a small couch through the doorway and hauled it next to her.

Once he'd retrieved the candle from the office, he picked through the pile of discarded clothes and selected a velvety dress-up cape and a long cardigan that would've fallen to Mel's knees had she worn it. He draped the cape over the couch and laid the sweater on the back of the chair.

"I'll take the chair," he said. "You can move to the

couch.”

“Are you sure?” She looked from Jaylen to the chair and back to him. There was no way he’d be comfortable sleeping there. “You’re so much taller than me.”

“I’ll be fine.” He brushed her off. “You should elevate your ankle overnight.”

Mel yawned again, too weary to argue. The couch did look inviting. She settled onto it, tucking her feet into the cardigan she had used earlier. Then, she lay on her uninjured side and pulled the velvet cape tight around her body. It had the same musty smell as the other clothes, but it would help to keep her warm as the library was sure to get cold overnight without any way to heat it.

“Are you tired enough to sleep?” she asked Jaylen.

It felt early to be going to sleep. At her cabin, she might have stayed up to read by firelight. She yawned yet again, and he chuckled.

“Good night, Mel.”

He blew out the candles and cloaked them in darkness. Mel was used to the dark, but she was used to it in the familiar, safe space of her home. Even though she couldn’t see the difference, she felt it. An unsettling flutter formed in her chest.

“Good night, Jaylen,” Mel whispered.

She heard him sit in the chair. There was a bit of creaking as he moved about, and then it grew quiet.

Once again, Mel was acutely aware of how different things felt here. In the cabin, she was often serenaded to sleep. In the summer, it was by crickets and peepers, and in the winter, by the scratching of branches in the wind. Now that the rain had stopped, the walls of the library kept the other night noises out, lending an oppressiveness to the quiet.

But Jaylen was there. She listened as his breathing grew steady. For her part, she struggled to keep her own breathing steady as her nose grew tingly and tears prickled the corner of her eyes.

Mel squeezed her eyes tight against the tears and let out a wavering breath. It was the closest she had slept to another person since the last night she had spent with her husband. She sniffled quietly and hoped the exhaustion would send her to sleep before the emotions overtook her.

CHAPTER 16

As soon as the light began to creep into the library, Mel and Jaylen were up and getting ready to head back to the cabin. There wasn't much to do except put the library back in order and pack up their stuff. She left the heavy-lifting of the furniture to Jaylen and focused on the small things.

She organized the clothes, putting hers in one pile and Jaylen's in another. Her jeans were stiff but dry everywhere except for the fabric around the zipper. She slipped them right over the leggings from the confiscated clothes.

She packed their silly accessories back into the tote they had come from, smiling as she placed Jaylen's flower crown on top. He carried the tote and his own clothes to the office. He came back in his regular clothes. Mel immediately missed the purple sequins on the jacket. She might have nicked the jacket, but she couldn't justify keeping something that served so little purpose.

She did, however, keep the owl cardigan. It fit her well and was warm. A good wash would remove the mustiness. As she pulled on her sweater from the day before, her side barely stung at all. The road rash had been superficial wounds, nothing a good cleaning and a slather of aloe from her plant wouldn't mend.

The book she had started the day before, though a bit on the creepy side, had been tucked into her backpack. It had effectively hooked her, and she had to know what secrets those women in the cabin were keeping.

The rest had been good for her ankle. As she pulled on her socks and slightly damp sneakers, she noted the swelling was down. Though, as she had suspected, the dark purple bruising had spread. That would probably take some time before it looked back to normal.

When Jaylen offered her a piece of goose jerky, Mel didn't even make a face. She simply shoved the whole thing in her mouth and chewed away. Only when it was mostly done did she gulp down the last of the water she had brought.

Back in the cabin, there were only a couple of mason jars of water left. If Jaylen didn't get the pump working today, she would have to seriously start thinking about alternative water sources. The lake was probably too far away for daily usage, but there was a stream that ran through the woods not too far from her property. Maybe she could figure out something with that. Jaylen might have some good ideas.

One thing at a time, she reminded herself. She could worry about water sources if, and only if, it became a long-term problem.

Packed and ready, they set off on the bikes toward the turn-off at the Thirsty Crow Tavern. Jaylen was ahead of her, carrying the extra burden of the backpack. The roads were damp but not puddled, and the skies were clear. The smells and sounds of the season were everywhere as early spring flowers scented the air and bird song serenaded them.

They proceeded slowly as Mel tested how her ankle was holding up. It was stiffer than usual and there was some pain, but it was bearable. The real test would come when they reached the hill. She built up as much speed as she felt comfortable with as they approached the hill, Jaylen in the lead. Mel leaned in and pumped her legs as best as she could to keep the momentum going for as long as possible. She downshifted to make the pedaling less strenuous.

Eventually, she ran out of steam and the bike slowly came to a halt. Ahead of her, Jaylen glanced back and stopped as well.

"Keep going." She waved him on.

"You sure?" he asked.

"Yes!" She tried not to show how out of breath she was. The ride up the hill was never easy, but today it felt insurmountably hard. She wouldn't slow him down.

He gave her a cute little wave. "See ya up there!"

Mel found herself smiling at the way his subtle accent, finding it more charming than ever.

He proceeded up the hill and before long, was out of sight. Mel began the slow hike herself, pushing along her bike. She stopped often for a rest and to gently roll her ankle to keep it from tightening up altogether. How she wished she hadn't drank all her water.

Slow and steady was the way to go…just like that story of the little engine she read to her class every year during her lesson about resilience. Even as she grew sweaty trudging up the hill, she daydreamed of a hot cup of tea. It was how she started each day.

Having Jaylen around had thrown some excitement into her life, to be sure. But the various injuries plaguing her body was an indication that excitement wasn't necessarily a good thing. She liked her routine. It kept her motivated; the mundane work of each day kept her alive. Without routine and planning, she was sure she be another dead body along with all the rest of the world. Well, all the rest of the world except for Jaylen.

The mystery of his life and circumstances prickled at her. Maybe over dinner, she could ask a few nonchalant questions and begin to put the pieces together. She told herself her curiosity over him wasn't so much about liking him as it a safety matter. Safety was also an important pillar of survival.

So what that she was picturing him in his sequined jacket and flower crown, a teasing smile on his face. That was simply a distraction to get her home.

Finally, she made the last push up the hill and turned the bike down her driveway all the way to the shed. She took a moment to catch her breath. While she did, she looked around at the cabin and property with fresh eyes.

She wondered what Jaylen thought of it all. Parts were shabbier looking than she realized, like the old pickup truck, whose tires had sunken into the ground. Weeds grew up around it. Soon, the wildflower meadow on the far side of the garden would be filled with flowers of all colors, bees and butterflies dancing among them. Right now, however, it was sparse and patchy as the plants grew in.

Her vegetable garden was coming along, the tilled earth and plantings in their neat lines and carefully counted rows. The peas were growing tall on their stakes and would hopefully begin to flower soon. She could almost feel the pop of a pod in her mouth and the sweetness of the tender peas inside.

The chicken coops were haphazard, given that she had built them herself. But they served the purpose of keeping the hens and Gilbert from wandering off. There was nothing wrong with utility over beauty.

The cabin itself had been newly finished with wood siding shortly after she and Daniel had bought the place. The siding on the sunny side of the house had begun to take on a silver-gray tone, while the north side retained its brown shade. The porch with its chairs and planters and hanging wind chimes was quite inviting. All in all, she was proud of what she had built here.

She loved this place she called home.

Chapter 17

Thankfully, all Mel had to do when she got home was take care of herself. All the rain the day before meant she didn't have to worry about watering the plants. Which was a relief because that meant she didn't have to worry about gathering water. With any luck, Jaylen would have the pump fixed today and she wouldn't have to worry about water for a long time.

She was looking forward to resting her ankle. But first, there was the matter of making tea. The water it required was well worth it because she was barely functional before she had her tea. She was well overdue after traversing the road home this morning.

Hobbling across the porch, she gathered ingredients. Chamomile and rosemary were first on her list because she was pretty sure they contained anti-inflammatory properties. Once inside, she shaved off a piece of ginger root and then set the water to boil on the stove.

Next up was to thoroughly clean the wound on her side, which required yet more water...and vodka. Tucked away in the pantry on the same shelf as the wine were a few bottles each of vodka and whiskey. She cracked open one of the vodka bottles.

Mel contemplated taking a swig but then thought better of it. Though it would help with the pain, she needed a clear head for what she was about to do. She sprinkled a little vodka on a washcloth, decided that wasn't enough, and soaked a large section of the cloth with the alcohol.

When she patted the wound with the vodka-soaked washcloth, she let out a sharp hiss as her side burned. Her head swam with dizziness for a minute. When that passed, she inspected the wound and found it looking less red and angry.

Next, it was time to prepare the aloe. Two aloe vera plants stood on the bookshelf in the corner by the bed where the window offered light but not direct sunlight, perfect for the medicinal plants.

She snipped off a thick spear down to the base because she needed a lot of aloe. Tipping the spear upside down, she let the yellowish liquid drain from it into the washcloth. The liquid contained a toxin that was a skin irritant, and it caused diarrhea. Not draining the toxin was a mistake she made only once before reading up on the proper way to use aloe.

The teakettle squealed to let her know the water was ready, so she made her tea while she waited for the aloe spear to stop leaking. The hot water struck a satisfying timbre as it streamed over the herbs in the infuser and into the mug. She let that steep and checked on the aloe.

It was ready, so she retrieved her sharp filleting knife, the one she used for fish, and went to work on the aloe spear. She trimmed off the top and pointed edges and cut the spear into sections. She set all but one aside. That one, she filleted, taking off the top skin. Now came the fun part.

With a spoon, she scooped the sticky center of the plant onto a glass cutting board. Mel took off her shirt and slathered the gel all over her wounded side. It provided an instant cooling sensation that made her sigh with relief. She let it dry for a few minutes before slipping on a clean t-shirt.

She spent the rest of the day on her couch with her foot elevated. She escaped back into the thriller book from the library. It didn't feel so scary reading it in the light of day. She only felt a little guilty that Jaylen spent his day working on her water pump while she loafed around. Rest was important, too.

As darkness began to fall, Mel prepared dinner. She had a couple of eggs from the other day in a bowl on the counter top that would be enough for two big omelets. She cracked those open and added fresh chive, basil, and parsley. Her pickled vegetables were running a bit low, but she had one jar of jalapenos she had been saving for a special occasion.

Today felt like a good day to open that last jar and give the omelets a little kick. She chopped up several jalapenos and tossed them into the scrambled eggs with the herbs. She hoped Jaylen liked spicy food.

The eggs needed one last thing. She looked around the kitchen and her gaze fell on the garlic bulbs hanging in a dark corner. That would be her final ingredient, along with a pinch of salt. She had raided many a supermarket for salt, but she was always careful to ration it. The process of how one made salt was something she knew nothing about. Did you even make salt? Harvest it? Certainly it wasn't grown. Was it? She didn't even know that much!

She was heating up the pan when she heard a knock. She limped to the door and opened it to find Jaylen smiling at her, though his eyes looked a little pinched with fatigue.

Mel had thought about checking on him earlier in the

day, but she had been so cozy on the couch, she hadn't wanted to get up. It wasn't often this time of year that she had an excuse to lounge around all day. Those kinds of days were for winter, not spring. Guilt crept at the edges of her contentment.

"Dinner is almost ready," she said.

"Great." His smile widened into the one that Mel found made her heart beat a little faster. "Can I help with anything?"

"No!" she practically shouted.

She didn't need to feel more guilt by having him help with dinner when she had done nothing all day. Besides, she wasn't sure she wanted to invite him into her home. They had shared some nice moments over the last few days, but she didn't really know him all that well. Plus, she and Daniel had been fixing up this cabin together, and she wasn't ready to share it with anyone else just yet.

She gently shoved him toward the porch. "Just relax. I'll bring out dinner in about fifteen minutes. Do you like spicy food?"

"Why yes I do, ma'am," he said, his accent particularly thick.

There was no remorse when she whacked him on the arm, her swat barely impacting the tight muscles beneath his shirt.

"You fiend," she accused.

He let out a deep laugh, the merriment in his eyes cutting through the tiredness. "Yes, ma'am, I am."

"Go relax." She shooed him away and shut the door.

The pan was piping hot and ready for the omelets. They cooked quickly, and soon, she was heading out with dinner. Jaylen had lit the candles from the other night, so it was bright and cheerful on the porch. She handed over one of the plates.

"Vegetable omelets. Sadly, no cheese."

"Smells good." He cut a piece and gently blew on it before taking a bite and chewing thoughtfully. "Delicious even without the cheese."

Mel took a bite with a big chunk of jalapeno in it. Tasty, she thought as she ate it, but a gooey Gruyere would have put it over the top. They ate in quiet companionship as the stars came out. Mel scraped up her last bite and bent down to set her plate on the ground. That's when she noticed a case leaning against the railing.

"Is that your guitar?" she asked.

"It is." There was no hint of fatigue when his gaze met hers.

"Will you play me something?"

He stood and deftly took the guitar out of the case. "I know just the song."

CHAPTER 18

Jaylen leaned against the porch railing and strummed the guitar. A discordant sound came out of it, and he grimaced.

"Out of tune," he explained. "I haven't played in awhile."

He began alternately plucking the strings and adjusting the knobs. Mel didn't know much about playing guitar, but she could at least figure out that he was tuning it.

She leaned back into the rocking chair and closed her eyes. It was like dessert for ears that had been existing solely on broccoli—her least favorite vegetable and one she never bothered growing—and he wasn't even playing a real song yet. It had been so long since she'd heard music, never mind live music! She wanted to soak it in.

Jaylen gave the guitar a final strum and even to Mel's untrained ear, she could tell it was tuned. She waited for a song to start, but the guitar remained silent.

When she opened her eyes to see what was happening, Jaylen was openly staring at her. He didn't balk at being caught, as she thought he ought to, but simply tilted his head and offered her a smile. Heat rose in her cheeks and her throat grew dry. She swallowed. They stayed staring at each other a moment, candlelight dancing between them, bringing out the red tones in his skin. She hoped her face didn't look too pale and hollow in the lowlight.

"Ready?" he finally asked.

She nodded, afraid her voice would give away how much he disarmed her.

She studied him as he strummed a few notes, his attention fully on the music now. They plucked at something in the back of her mind. The tune felt familiar like she should know it, but she couldn't quite place it.

He played another minute, glancing up expectantly with the unspoken question of whether she knew what he was playing. She shrugged, still not recognizing it. He pointedly paused his playing, and when he started back up he sang, adding his deep voice to the guitar.

It took less than two lines for her to finally place it. She knew it well, but the original was played on the piano, not the guitar, and it had been so long since she'd last heard it. The title finally pushed through to Mel's mind.

"Cardigan!" She tugged at the owl cardigan from the library. The musty smell was wearing off, so she had thrown it on to come out to dinner. She would wash it on the next laundry day, which was at least another week away.

With a big grin on her face, Mel swayed in her seat as Jaylen played and sang. His voice was so much deeper than Taylor Swift's, so it was like listening to a whole new song. One that was just for them. They had an inside joke now, no matter that there was no one else in the world to not be in on the joke.

There could have been a million people around and that song would still have been a special moment between the two of them, immortalizing their night in the library with cardigans and a purple-sequined jacket.

When the last note rang out and Jaylen fell quiet, Mel jumped up and clapped. She let out a loud "woooo!" like she was at a rock concert.

He bowed with a flourish. "Thank you. Thank you."

She hoped he would play some more. Not having music in her life for so long was a void she hadn't known was there. It created a tingle in her body and a warmth in her heart. Now that it was back, she wanted more of it.

"You played that from memory?" she asked.

"I had to adjust the key to fit my voice, but yeah." His gaze fell on the guitar as his face fell. "My fiancé was a bit of a Swiftie."

It was the most personal thing he had shared since she'd met him. She sensed he didn't want to talk about it further, so she hastily said, "It's kind of not fair that you're smart and musically inclined."

That brought his signature smile to his face. "You think I'm smart?"

She widened her eyes playfully. "You're an aerospace engineer. You know you're smart."

"I like hearing you say it." He smirked. Then, more seriously, he said, "Music isn't really that different from engineering."

She shot him an incredulous look.

He shook his head and looked down at the guitar. "No, really. A lot of it is about patterns. The big difference with music is that it's better when you bring a piece of your soul to it."

There was no arguing with that.

"Can you play another song, Mr. Smarty-pants?"

He cleared his throat and looked up at her. "Yeah. Let me think a minute."

She watched his face go from forlorn to thoughtful as he

silently moved his fingers on the strings while mouthing some words.

"Okay," he said. "I've got one."

He launched into a rock song that Mel recognized but didn't know the name of. She chimed in on the chorus the second time through, despite being off-key. She clapped once again when he finished.

This time, he didn't hesitate to start another. It was soulful and older than the other two. Mel was pretty sure she had never heard it before. Jaylen's voice wavered over the last note, and he played the song to the end with a sad look in his eyes.

"My mama used to sing that one to us when we were kids," he said quietly.

"It's beautiful."

He nodded thoughtfully, staring at some point past her head. He seemed lost in the past until he shook his head and smiled at her. She smiled back in what she hoped was a reassuring way. She knew how easy it was to slip into a depression over the past.

"Do you think I could borrow the bike again tomorrow?" he asked abruptly, effectively ending the concert. "I need a few more things from the hardware store."

"Yeah, of course." Not wanting to act like he owed her anything, Mel had been waiting for him to bring up the progress on the water pump, but now seemed a good time to outright ask. "How's the repair coming along?"

"Good," he said as he put his guitar back in the case. "I should be able to test it out tomorrow, and hopefully it'll be back up and running."

"That's great." She hesitated, finding her conversational skills had turned awkward again. "I really appreciate you helping me out."

"No problem. Don't feel like you have to come along this time. Your ankle probably needs more rest before another bike trip."

"Yeah, that's fine. For you to go alone, I mean." Her cheeks flamed with embarrassment as she tried to let him know it was no big deal for him to go alone. "I have things I need to do around here, anyway."

The last line had come out kind of begrudgingly without her meaning it that way. Dinner and the music had been so magical, and now she was acting like she had a shoe stuck in her mouth. Jaylen had even shared a few personal details. How had she managed to turn this beautiful night into something so awkward?

"I should get some sleep," he said. "I want to get an early start tomorrow."

"Of course."

Avoiding eye contact, she picked up the dishes as he blew out the candles. She thought she heard him say "good night" as she opened the cabin door. When she turned around to return the sentiment, he was lost to the darkness.

She went inside, shut the door behind her, and leaned up against it heavily. A strange mix of emotions swirled around inside her. They stayed with her as she tucked herself into bed.

Usually it was sadness, loneliness, or a combination of the two that kept her up at night. This time, it was curiosity over Jaylen mixed with regret of how they'd ended the night...and something else. A thing she hadn't felt in a long time, something she wasn't expected to ever feel again. Something she wasn't ready to put a name to, not yet anyway.

Chapter 19

Mel woke to a sound that made her happy: the caw of the crows. She leapt out of bed, the chill of the floor hitting her bare feet with a shock she ignored, to look out the window.

A murder of crows sat along the low branches of their usual morning resting spot on the evergreen that overlooked the henhouse. Their caws were the soft chirping ones that meant they wanted Mel to feed them, not the harsh calls when they sensed danger. She thought back to when she had last seen them at breakfast, and it had to have been a week.

She had been so busy with the water pump and Jaylen that she hadn't even noticed the birds' absence, which normally would have been cause for concern. No matter, they were back and she was delighted to see them.

Mel hurried off to get ready. After stoking the wood stove, she opened her last jar of fresh water and poured half of it in the kettle. It would only be enough to make a small mug of tea, but it would have to do. If Jaylen didn't get the pump working today, she would plan on going to the river tomorrow. It would mean having to boil the water for drinking, cooking, and the dishes, but she couldn't go any longer without it.

She went about gathering the same anti-inflammatory ingredients as yesterday. It seemed to have worked for her ankle, so she was eager to keep at it. Once the tea water boiled, she poured it over the herbs to let it steep while she got ready.

The cabin had a chill about it this morning, so that meant it would be cold outside. She put on warm socks, a sweater, and a jacket. As she shoved her feet into her boots, her injured ankle smarted just a little. It was well on its way to being healed.

There wasn't much food prepared that would suit the birds. Mel hadn't baked anything since before the trip to the hardware store. She grabbed seeds for the chickens and what was left of the cornbread from several days ago for the crows. The bread was probably stale, but the crows didn't tend to be picky.

She walked down the porch steps as fast as she could without spilling her tea, before slowing as she reached the henhouse, so as not to scare the birds. She scattered the seeds in Gilbert's and the hen's pens.

The hens came strutting out of the house, Rachel Lynde leading the way, and began pecking at the seeds. Marilla was the last one out, but there was still plenty for her to eat. Gilbert the rooster had yet to make an appearance over in his coop. Usually his crowing roused her from sleep and all the birds got an early breakfast, so maybe he was pouting about how late Mel had come out.

Next, she approached the pine tree. The crows ceased their cawing, and she clicked her tongue in greeting.

"Good morning," she said in a sing-songy voice.

One crow cocked its head toward her in an expectant way. Its black feathers looked sleek in the sunlight. She broke the last of the cornbread into pieces and tossed them at the base of the tree. The crows swooped down on them a few at a time, the rest staying on their perches to watch. This was the way of the crows, always looking out for each other.

While the birds ate, Mel sat in one of the Adirondack chairs and sipped her tea. Steam rose out of the mug and warmed her nose, an earthy scent rising up with it.

Gilbert finally made an appearance. She watched him strut around the pen and thought of what she needed to do, not only today but over the next few days and weeks. She tried not to think too far ahead because the list became too long and she got overwhelmed. There was always something ahead that needed to be done.

One of the things she wanted to do this summer was to try and breed one of the hens with Gilbert. She had decided this after losing Josie Pye over the winter. A lifespan of five to ten years was typical, so these hens were all in their old age. If she didn't breed more soon, she risked there being no more eggs.

She was better with plants than animals, so it was a feat she wasn't necessarily looking forward to. But summertime was the time for breeding, according to her research, so it was worth a try.

Mel's stomach grumbled with hunger as she took her last sip of tea. The cornbread was gone, and the crows had dispersed. Gilbert had disappeared into his little house again, and the hens were clucking about as they finished the seeds.

There was no sign of Jaylen anywhere. She supposed he must've headed to the hardware store already. She stretched and headed back to the cabin for breakfast.

They had finished up the jar of blueberry jam the other night, so she opened a strawberry one. It was very satisfying to pop the seal on each new jar of jam, though it was always a reminder of the limited resources available. She scooped out a few spoonfuls as she took stock of how many full jars were left in the pantry. It wasn't very many, but it would be strawberry season again soon.

She made a mental note to check on her supply of empty canning jars. The jars weren't so much the problem because she could wash those. It was the sealing lids that were limited. She had acquired as many as she could back when she had access to a vehicle. But once those lids were gone, that was it.

There was always something at risk of running out. Whether that be lids for the jam jars or eggs from the hens. This was the way of survival.

With a sigh, Mel got to work for the day, tending her plants and taking care of the things she had control over. She tried not to think too hard about what she didn't have and hoped that by the end of the day, water wouldn't be one of those things.

Chapter 20

Jaylen was gone most of the day. Mel was busy in the garden, so she hardly noticed. But she did notice a little, which was strange.

A few days with another person and already she missed him when he was gone. Not in the sob in bed kind of way, of course, which was the way she had missed Daniel. That was the missing of grief. She missed Jaylen in a nice to have a friend kind of way.

It was nice to have someone to look out for her besides herself. Though, it scared her the way she could get used to it. She wouldn't allow that.

Beyond fixing her water pump, Jaylen had said nothing about what his plans were, but she couldn't imagine he meant to stick around. Not that she necessarily wanted that. Yeah, not getting used to him being around was the way to go, no matter how much she thought of him while he was gone.

She took her feelings out on the soil, throwing her energy into spearing the earth with the hoe again and again. She turned the soil in a patch of garden where she would plant her tomato saplings. Last night had been cold, but it was well past the danger of frost. That meant the warm weather plants would be ready to go in soon.

Summer was her favorite time of year where a variety of fresh food was abundant. The days were long and there was much to do, but that also meant less time to sit and think.

Winter was a quiet time of reflection, and Mel always felt sadder in the winter. She retreated to books, but having to be still and inside so much meant her mind wandered to places she didn't want it to go. Maybe it was the lack of sunlight, or maybe life was just hard and it was better to be busy and not think about it.

Jaylen arrived as Mel was wrapping up her work in the garden. She had grown warm and thirsty, which had made her a little crabby.

Nevertheless, she smiled brightly when she saw him heading down the driveway on the bike. Then, she was annoyed with herself at how her mood brightened at seeing him, and that made her crabby again.

He waved and rode right to the shed to put the bike away. She waved back, more emotions swirling around inside her. It felt like the time before she had been diagnosed with adenomyosis and everything made her want to hit something. Of course, she hadn't gone around hitting things; she had just felt that way. But that hadn't been a problem since her hysterectomy.

They exchanged nods as they passed each other, Mel on her way to the cabin and Jaylen headed to the water pump, his backpack slung over one shoulder.

She cleaned up as best she could without water and thought about dinner. Lentils were out since they needed a lot of liquid to cook. Salad was boring and not terribly filling.

Her stomach rumbled with hunger as if to prove she needed more than greens for dinner. She balked at making more eggs, but the protein would be good for them both.

She stomped her foot like a child and let out a cry of frustration. Everything was so much harder without water.

She ended up frying the eggs over medium and serving greens on the side. A week ago, she wouldn't have thought twice about making this, but she was now in a constant state of second-guessing everything she did. This was not how she operated. Why was it so hard to just be herself now that someone else was around?

Jaylen wasn't there waiting for her on the porch when she brought the food out, so she took the meal to him. Eggs weren't very good once they got cold, and she wasn't going to let him ruin her meal.

He was working on something inside the control box when she arrived.

He turned around when he heard her coming with a surprised look. "Dinner already?"

It wasn't quite dark yet, so maybe she was a little earlier than usual with the food. Then again, it was staying lighter later each day, so maybe she was right on time. She refused to blame herself for not being accommodating enough. She was hungry and wanted to eat now. Why should she work around his schedule?

Because he's helping you, a little voice in her head reminded her. She grumbled low enough that he didn't hear her...or he was polite enough to ignore it.

She held out one of the plates. "I didn't want the eggs to get cold."

"Thanks." He wiped his hands on a towel. "Meet you in our usual spot in a few?"

Mel nodded and pulled the plate back in. She didn't

recognize the towel as one of hers, so it must have been his. It made sense that he would have a towel, but for some reason, she was annoyed at how much stuff he had managed to fit in his bags. She wondered how he traveled when he had so much stuff with him.

Stomping more than walking, she headed to the porch with the food. Come to think of it, she had no idea where that man slept at night. Did he have a tent as well? Where had he set it up?

She placed Jaylen's plate on his chair—no, her chair that he sometimes sat in. She didn't wait for him to arrive before stuffing a piece of romaine in her mouth. Maybe she was hangry and the food would help her feel better.

She poked the egg and watched the yellow yolk seep out. With her fork, she pushed the greens into the gooey yolk and mixed it around like a dressing. It was just warm enough to wilt the greens but not take all the crunch out of them, and it was quite yummy.

"Looks good," Jaylen said, startling her.

She shrugged and barely kept her eyes from rolling as he sat. He always said that about her food.

"Are you okay, Mel?" he asked.

There was that question again. As if she had ever been okay in the last five years.

"I'm just tired," she said—true but not the whole truth. "And probably dehydrated."

She scooped up the last bite of food and still felt unsatisfied as she finished. She eyed Jaylen's half-full plate.

"Why don't you go in and try the tap?" he said.

She felt her mood perk up a little. "It's ready?"

"There's only one way to know."

She went inside without inviting him in. He was probably better off not being in her company right now, especially if he hadn't delivered on the water. Not that she was ready to invite him into her cabin anyway.

With a deep breath of hope, she twisted the handle on the kitchen sink. Something under the sink made a deep echoing kind of noise. Then, nothing happened.

She was about to turn off the tap and deliver the bad news to Jaylen when a stream of water shot out. It ran brown for a minute before clearing.

Mel's mouth watered. She didn't bother with a glass, but simply stuck her mouth right into the stream, lapping the water up like a dog. Once she had her fill, she ran out to the porch.

Jaylen leaned against the railing as he'd done when playing the guitar. Without thinking, she loped across the porch and wrapped her arms around him.

"You're amazing!"

All of a sudden, the warmth of his body hit her. She realized she was hugging him and quickly pulled away, her throat dry again.

"Jaylen," she said with more reserve. "Thank you."

He stared at her, something behind the piercing gaze that put a pause on Mel's happiness. Then, worry began to kick in. Was it only a temporary fix? Was something else wrong with the water pump?

"What is it?" she whispered.

Jaylen frowned and rubbed his beard. "There's something I need to tell you."

Chapter 21

Based on the way Jaylen's forehead pinched in distress, Mel was guessing the thing he had to tell her was not good news. That irritable feeling that had lingered inside Mel all day long pushed its way toward panic.

A million thoughts on what the bad news could be flashed through her mind. Maybe the water pump was only temporarily fixed and it would fully break down soon, leaving her without a reliable water source. Or there was a dangerous bacteria in the water and now she was going to die from drinking it. Or something that had nothing to do with the water but was still a threat to her life.

Maybe it was something as simple as him moving on now that he'd helped her. Which wasn't nearly as catastrophic as the other things but made her sad all the same.

Panic tightened her throat. She took a deep breath, not really wanting to know but needing to stop the spiraling thoughts. "What is it?"

"There's something I haven't told you," he said.

He looked away as if it pained him to see her face. She

was sure the worry and panic were showing on it. Her heart beat so hard, she could feel it in her throat, which only caused it to tighten up even more.

"I have a vehicle," he said, the words not living up to the emotions threatening to choke Mel.

She coughed. "A vehicle?" she said stupidly. "Like a car? That works?"

He nodded, making brief eye contact before looking away again. "It's a pickup truck. That's how I got here. It broke not far from your cabin. I wasn't sure if I would be able to fix it, so I didn't bother to mention it before now. But I found the parts I needed at the hardware store today, so it's up and running again."

She was a little annoyed at just finding out about the truck, but it wasn't like it could've helped them earlier when it had been broken. It's not like she would've been able to avoid the accident with the bike. He had needed to get to the hardware store, and they had needed the bikes to do that.

None of that was as bad as the things she had imagined. Her mind reasoned all this out, yet it still hurt that Jaylen had kept this secret.

Sure, there were many things Mel hadn't told him. There were things that were irrelevant to anything they had done or talked about. There were things that were too personal to talk about with a man she had only known for a handful of days.

Somehow, though, the secret of the truck didn't fit either of those categories. It would have been natural for him to bring up the truck when they were at the hardware store, and having a truck wasn't too personal to share. So why the secrecy and the guilty demeanor while telling her?

Instead of asking what she really wanted to know, she said, "I haven't been able to get my pickup started in ages.

Where did you find gas for it?"

Jaylen's mouth lifted in a pleased little grin. "It doesn't run on gas. It's solar-powered."

That caught her off-guard and muted the panicked reaction. "How did you get a solar-powered truck?"

His grin grew bigger.

"Wait," she said. "Don't tell me you built one?"

"It was more like putting the right pieces together to get solar panels to run an electric-powered truck."

"Wow!" Mel knew Jaylen was smart, but creating a solar-powered truck, that was impressive.

His face turned solemn again. "Are you mad at me for not telling you?"

"No."

The secrecy and the resulting panic it had induced were upsetting, but it wasn't like her reaction was all his fault. Some of it was ingrained in who she was and the trauma she had endured. Besides, how could she be mad over such a trivial matter when he had helped her so much?

"It's okay," she said. "I'm okay."

To her surprise, Jaylen was still subdued after her reassurances. She couldn't guess about what. Their histories were tragedies, and something that seemed simple to her could bring up a whole host of feelings in him. Maybe this truck somehow reminded him of his past. Who was she to judge him for that?

And maybe there was a way to turn this into a happy moment.

"We should take a road trip," she declared.

He opened his mouth, but before he could say no, she added, "A short one. There's a place nearby that I've always wanted to visit, but I never got the chance to. It's too far for the bike, but it would make the perfect day trip if we drive."

He stared at her quizzically. This bout of spontaneity was out of character for Mel, so much so that even a man she had only known for days could figure that out.

She wasn't sure where it was coming from. Maybe she was tired of playing it safe and carefully calculating every move of her life. Now that she had the security of running water again, she felt freed up to do something different. It was just one day after all.

"I'm running low on firewood. We can scavenge for it along the way. I never took a car up that way. I'm sure we can find a house with a stockpile of it. It'll save me the trouble of having to cut wood."

"You sure?"

The probing way his eyes roved over her face made her wonder what he was thinking. Maybe he didn't realize how out of character this was for her.

"I'm sure," she said more confidently than she felt.

"Okay, ma'am." A grin split his face, and she rolled her eyes. "Where are we going?"

"The Olympic Center at Lake Placid."

She had no idea what kind of condition it would be in, but it was a place she and Daniel had always wanted to go. He'd grown up playing hockey and had been obsessed with the Miracle on Ice game when the U.S. beat the Soviet Union and later went on to win the gold medal at the Olympics.

They'd watched all the movies about it multiple times. They had planned on visiting the Olympic Center after they finished the cabin, neither of which had happened.

She'd finally get to see the place of miracles. It would be with a different man than she had planned, but she would do this for her late husband and have the adventure they never got to have together.

CHAPTER 22

Other than the large solar panels in the bed of the truck, riding in Jaylen's self-made solar vehicle wasn't much different than riding in a gas-powered pickup. He explained the top cruising speed was considerably lower than what Mel had been used to in the before-times, but the driving was all on back routes anyway, so the lack of speed wasn't noticeable.

Dust covered the black exterior just as it did her old pickup, only Jaylen's truck was much bigger. The bed was bigger, which was necessary to accommodate the solar panels, but the cab was also bigger as it had a full backseat. She peered into the backseat to see it full of supplies, which explained why Jaylen seemed so self-sufficient when he arrived. He had everything he needed for the trip right in this vehicle.

Mel used her trusty atlas of New York road maps to direct them to the Olympic Center. It was less than an hour from when they left to when they pulled up right in front of the arena. They sat there a moment, Jaylen seemingly waiting for her to take the lead.

A line of flagpoles jutted out of a walkway opposite the arena. Mel guessed they had once held the flags of many nations, but all that was left were tattered remains, too torn and faded to identify. Down a small hill was an overgrown grassy area that once housed an outdoor speed skating rink.

The arena building was largely comprised of windows. It was rather impressive and modern-looking, even with the grime that had accumulated over years of neglect. Most impressive about it, though, was that the glass was all still intact.

"Do you want to go in?" Jaylen asked.

She hadn't bothered to explain why she'd wanted to visit the Olympic Center, and she hadn't planned what she would do when they got here. Upon seeing all that glass, a seed of something dangerous was planted inside her. She wanted to go inside, and she wanted to make a ruckus doing it.

"Find a rock." She shot him a fiendish look as she exited the truck.

She searched the surrounding area and found a rock the size of a grapefruit. Jaylen procured an even bigger one, which upon closer inspection proved not to be a rock but a chunk of broken concrete.

Standing in front of one of the big glass windows, Mel held the rock like it was a shot put ball, ready to toss it. Jaylen picked up on what she planned to do and stood in front of the window next to her.

"Are you sure?" he asked. "It could be dangerous."

All she said in response was "on the count of three" and counted down.

They tossed their projectiles. Her rock hit the glass with a thud and bounced off. His concrete chunk, however, smashed right through the glass, which shattered in a million little pieces upon impact.

"I should've used a bigger rock," she said, her eyebrows arched in amusement.

The tiny pieces of glass crunched under their shoes as they approached the entrance Jaylen had made for them and peered inside.

"I feel a little bad," he said. "This glass was standing the test of time, enduring without anyone here to take care of it."

It was a thought Mel might have shared on a different occasion. But ever since yesterday—no, before that really, since the rainstorm when she had gone flying off her bike—she had been feeling restless. The care and caution she put into every day of her life weighed on her. She was like a sheltered teenager leaving home for the first time. And she had a small taste of rebellion that sparked a want of more.

It wasn't the same unhinged desperation she had felt the day she drove all the way to Virginia. That was a dangerous, ugly feeling. Today, she simply felt free.

She stepped through the broken window, her boots crunching over the broken glass, to where the concrete slab had landed inside. It was covered in tiny bits of glass.

She carefully picked it up and shook it clean. Carrying it with both hands, she went back out of the building.

"Stand back," she instructed Jaylen, and he listened, moving away from the windows.

Mel swung the concrete back and hurled it at the window she had tried to break before. This time, the glass shattered.

She kind of wanted to break another window. But then she caught Jaylen watching her carefully. His cool expression revealed nothing of his emotions, but she got the feeling he was judging her actions and finding them a little unhinged.

She smiled in what she hoped was a sane way and

gestured to the gaps where the windows had been. "Shall we?"

"After you," he said.

Once more, she crunched over broken glass and entered the building, Jaylen following behind.

It had the usual musty smell of an old, unused building, but there was an extra funk about the place. It was a damp, watery stink that evoked nothing of fresh rain or a river. More like a swamp, but with none of the warmth. The place was strangely cool, a chill about the air that made it feel colder than the outside air.

Mel shivered. She fetched a candle from her bag and lit it.

They made their way through an entrance tunnel to the hockey rink. Once they reached the stands, there was virtually no natural light. The candle hardly allowed them to see much of the place, even as their eyes adjusted to the dark. That pervasive damp chill grew worse...as did the smell.

Mel wasn't sure what she had expected to find. A spark of emotion? A sense of awe?

Instead, all she felt was darkness hemming her in on all sides. There was a faint dripping sound coming from parts unknown. A staccato plop that could drive her mad if she stood there listening to it for too long. It reminded her of Edgar Allan Poe's "The Tell-Tale Heart" and the beating of the heart under the floorboards.

She gagged as she imagined dead bodies hidden by the darkness.

She turned and fled back out of the tunnel into the light without a word to Jaylen. He was right on her heels as she retreated into the fresh air.

He asked the same question he always seemed to be

asking of her. "Are you okay?"

"Stop asking me that!" she snapped. She took a few deep breaths and tried to calm herself. She channeled the calming corner she had created in her classroom and imagined rubbing her hands along a soft blanket. "Sorry. It's not like I thought it would be."

He made a low "hmm" in agreement. They stood there in silence. Jaylen patiently waiting while something dark stirred inside Mel. She wrapped her arms around herself, but she couldn't shake the chill that had taken hold.

"Was there something else you wanted to see?" he finally asked. "Or should we go home?"

She noted his use of the word "home" and wondered when he had started thinking of the cabin like that or if he was simply referring to it as her home.

"Not home," she said firmly. "There's one more place if you don't mind."

"I don't mind."

She looked around. Behind her was the hockey arena and in front of her was the speed skating rink. The thing she was looking for should have been conspicuous, but it was nowhere to be found.

"I wanted to see the ski jumps," she said, her voice high and broken. "I don't know where it is."

"C'mon, I'll help you find it."

He headed down the sidewalk toward a light-brown brick building adjacent to the arena. She followed, her throat thick with emotions she was afraid to name.

# CHAPTER 23

The brick building was adorned with the Olympic rings in white instead of their usual array of colors. There was another display of flagpoles with the same tattered remains as the ones across from the hockey rink. The place was feeling bleak, and the mission of finding what Mel had been looking for was feeling hopeless.

The building turned out to be the Olympic Museum. Jaylen smashed the glass doors with a loose brick and lead them inside. Rather listlessly, Mel followed him around until he stopped at the museum's gift shop.

"I'm going to look for a map," he said.

She shrugged, not caring if he saw or not.

The shop housed the typical tchotchke for tourists, like sweatshirts and mugs. Fitting with the theme of the museum, it also featured various hockey equipment: laces and guards for skates, mouth guards, those squeeze water bottle hockey players used. Reminded of Daniel, she quickly skirted that section.

It was the kind of place she normally would've explore to find supplies she hadn't thought of needing, or maybe to find a replacement for something that was wearing out. Today, she couldn't bring herself to care about the chance to stock up on supplies.

Mel ran her hand along a selection of alpine-themed winter hats. They were well-made, the kind of material that lasted a long time, but she wasn't thinking about that. Her head was lost in thoughts of what might have been. Thoughts she usually tucked away to a deep part of her brain because what was the point of imagining a future that could never have been?

Memories were one thing, bittersweet and often painful, but manageable in small doses. Projections of the future were something else entirely, forbidden because of their destructiveness. Allowing these thoughts in, all the millions of things Daniel had missed in life—and not just him but everyone she had ever known—was a terrible idea.

She'd been down that road before and it had nearly ended her; she didn't think she could come back another time. Yet, she couldn't stop the thoughts from flooding her mind.

Coming to a place that had been so important to Daniel, a place he never got to see, dislodged something within Mel.

She yanked a hat from the rack and rubbed the material between her fingers to try and control her errant thoughts. She closed her eyes and focused on the feel of the material in between her fingers and only that. She slowly came out of her head back into her body, grounding herself in the reality of being in the gift shop with a hat in her hands.

When she opened her eyes, Jaylen was staring at her patiently. He leaned against the counter that housed the cash register, an Olympic Center map laid out on top. He didn't ask if she was okay this time. It was clear that she wasn't.

"Hey," he said softly. "I found the ski jumps."

"Okay," she responded in a flat voice.

"It looks like it's too far to walk, but we could take the truck. Do you still want to go?"

His eyes were so kind as they took in her distressed state. It made her want to cry, but she swallowed back the sensation, afraid she'd never stop if she got started.

Her voice was hoarse when she said, "Yes."

"New hat?" He pointed at the hat in her hands, and she looked at it for the first time.

It was dark green with an off-white moose stitched on it, a matching pompom on the top. She nodded.

"I could use one, too." From the rack, he took a baby blue hat decorated with a white mountain and pulled it onto his head. Then, he found a light pink jacket that was far too small and attempted to get his arms into it. "I think they're my colors."

Once again, Jaylen's clothing antics were proving to be a much-needed distraction. While not entirely back to herself, she found a small smile playing at her lips. She shook her head and stretched onto her tippy toes to pluck the hat from his head.

She selected a burgundy one with a large wolf stitched on it in gray and held it out to him. "This one."

He reached out for it, but his arms were still stuck inside the too-small sleeves of the jacket and he couldn't reach it. He bent down instead for her to put it on him. The back of her fingers brushed the side of his face as she pulled the hat down over his hair. His cheek was warm to the touch.

He caught her hand under his and pinned it to his cheek. "Your hands are cold."

She hadn't realized she was cold until her skin had touched his. He moved her hand away from his face, holding it in between his hands and blowing on it for warmth before letting it go.

"Hang on," he said.

He shrugged out of the pink jacket, letting it fall to the floor and leaving it there. There was a pair of fuzzy mittens on the same display as the hats. He picked them up and easily yanked off the tags. Holding one mitten in his mouth, he gripped her wrist and slid the mitten on her hand. He repeated the gesture with the second mitten.

For a long moment, he stayed leaning forward, eyes level with hers, her hands firmly ensconced in between his.

"Thanks," she whispered.

"You're welcome," he whispered back.

She wanted to take a step back, but she also didn't want to. She settled for clearing her throat. He patted her hands one more time and stood to his full height.

"We should go soon if we want to get you back home before dark," he said.

This time, she noted Jaylen referencing the cabin specifically as her home.

Hands no longer cold but thoughts still scattered, she followed him out of the store and back to the truck.

CHAPTER 24

The drive to the ski jumps was only a handful of minutes, and Mel mostly stared at her mittens the entire time. Her hands were warm now, thanks to Jaylen's kind gesture, but her mind was still skating on the edge of that dangerous place.

When Jaylen stopped the truck, Mel was surprised to look up and see the looming ski jumps gracing the hill in front of them. He shot her a worried glance before exiting the truck. She hesitantly followed, a strange sensation building in her chest.

In silence, they walked past a building and to the edge of an overgrown area of wildflowers and grass. Bees and birds flitted around the bright flowers. She spotted a yellow swallowtail perched on a bud, though it felt too cold for butterflies and flowers. Or maybe she was just cold from the inside out.

Even with all the beauty in front of her, she hesitated to go farther as concerns about Lyme Disease filled her head. Any hiker in upstate New York knew disease-carrying ticks were rampant in the area and that it was wise to do a body check after being out in nature. She did this every day during the warmer months when she was outside a lot.

As she stood on the border of the wild meadow, she wondered when her life had become one of constant risk assessment. Sure, it made sense not to engage in anything too risky with there being no medicine, doctors, or hospitals anymore.

She dreaded having an accident or contracting an illness that would incapacitate her, leaving her to suffer from dehydration or exposure to the elements while slowly dying. There were some things—like food, water, and shelter—that required such vigilance, but did everything in her life need to be that way? There was a mental cost to constantly being in a state of worry, like not being able to enjoy the beauty of a field of wildflowers, a cost that seemed to be adding up.

With a sense of trepidation, Mel plunged into the meadow and came out the other end to an artificial surface. It rapidly sloped up a natural hill to the upper part of the jumps that jutted out of the surface of the hill on concrete pillars. The turf was a faded green, though parts of it were worn down to the dirt below.

Jaylen shielded his eyes from the bright sunlight as he stared up at the top of the jumps. He pointed to the defunct gondola cars swaying slightly in the mountain breeze. "Guess we'll have to walk."

The joke didn't land. Mel was too preoccupied with the trepidation that continued to build inside her.

She looked at the structures she had longed to see. Now that she was here, she wasn't sure what exactly had driven her to want to see them. Unlike the hockey rink, which had a direct connection to Daniel, the ski jumps felt more like a curiosity, a place they had talked about going to but not one with a particular significance.

With equal parts fear and desire, Mel began the hike up the turf hill and Jaylen followed. She was breathing heavily and had grown sweaty by the time she got to the base of the upper part of the jumps. The concrete pillars were larger than they had appeared from down below. The size of them pushing up toward the sky gave her a weird feeling in her stomach.

She pulled the mittens off her hands, which were now sweating, and shoved them into her jacket pockets. The wind blew the hair all about her face and she tucked it back behind her ears.

"I don't think we should climb any higher," came Jaylen's deep voice from right next to her. She jumped at his proximity. He was also winded after traversing the hill, and it was another minute before he caught his breath and said, "I don't trust those structures not to collapse if we go on them."

She had been thinking the same thing, but she was having a hard time trusting her judgment just now.

A closer inspection of the concrete supports showed they were actually elevators that once brought tourists to the top. Mel dared to crane her neck to peer all the way up to the top of them. It was like standing at the base of a skyscraper and looking straight up to find the world had tilted in an off-kilter way.

Her breath caught in her chest and her throat constricted. She took a step back as she struggled to breathe and bumped into something hard that stopped her quick.

It turned out to be Jaylen. He turned her around by the shoulders and took in her stricken state. Spots danced in her eyes, dotting her view of his face.

"Hey, hey," he said. "It's okay. Just breathe." He demonstrated by taking his own big breath and letting it out slowly. "Nice and deep."

She tried to do the same, but her breaths hitched and stuttered.

Nevertheless, he said, "That's right. Just breathe."

When her breathing evened out, she felt light-headed and leaned on his firm chest for support. He wrapped his arms around her, warm and comforting. She pressed her cheek to his jacket, the zipper biting into skin. She grounded herself in the pain.

The conflicting feelings that had been building inside her all day finally released as she sobbed against him.

Over the last four days, she'd had more breakdowns in front of this man than she'd had by herself in the last four years. That first year of being alone in the cabin had been full of them, or rather it had been like having one long breakdown that culminated in the big one of her road trip.

But her emotions had been stable for years now. That all seemed to be falling apart since Jaylen had shown up. It was equal parts embarrassing and comforting to have him here to share in this with her.

She stood on that hill, the jumps looming above her and the wind buffeting around her, and she wasn't alone anymore. She had no idea how long he would stay with her, but in that moment, she was glad to have his solid presence to cry on.

CHAPTER 25

Jaylen let her get it all out, keeping his arms around Mel as she sobbed. He rubbed her back gently until she quieted.

Reluctantly, she pulled out of his embrace and looked up at him sheepishly. "I'm a mess. I swear I'm not always like this."

"No need to swear on my account, ma'am." Jaylen winked, an actual real-life wink.

That sent Mel into an unhinged fit of giggles. She laughed so hard she bent over double, hands on her knees to support herself. When she straightened, Jaylen regarded her with a guarded expression.

"Told you," she said. "Total mess."

"Not a mess," he said. "A survivor. You're a survivor, Mel."

That declaration from him silenced her. There were a lot of things she wanted to say about her feelings on survivors, but mainly on how she had thought she was the only one for a very long time. Knowing she wasn't had thrown her emotions into turmoil.

"It's beautiful," Jaylen said seemingly out of the blue.

For a moment, Mel thought he was talking about her, but he'd said "it," so that didn't make sense. "What's beautiful?"

He made a sweeping gesture out in front of him. "The view."

It *was* beautiful, the mountains a dark blue against the bright sky and the trees lush with their spring green. A fresh breeze whipped at her hair. She inhaled deeply, taking in the cleansing air. Her energy was spent after the outburst, and she let the tranquility of the scene wash over her.

The calm didn't last long before an uneasy feeling rose in her chest.

"You're a survivor, too," she said. "And I don't see you having a breakdown every damn day."

Jaylen let out a harsh chuckle. "Believe me, I've had my moments. I imagine it's hard when you've been alone a long time and someone turns up and changes things."

She shot him a sharp look, not sure if he was talking about her or himself. His expression gave away nothing. He simply looked like a man taking in the sights. Had she thrown him for as much of a loop as he'd thrown her? He sure wasn't showing it if that was the case.

"We should head back down," he said. "The truck's lights take up too much juice for us to make it home with them on, and I don't want to drive on these mountain roads in the dark."

They hiked down the turf surface, Mel taking most of it side-footed because it was so steep. Her knees would be sore tomorrow. The hazards of being in her 40s. She had to think a moment before remembering her age—she would be 45, no, 46 this year.

She wondered yet again how old Jaylen was. She had already figured him to be younger, but by how much. She itched to ask him, but doing so felt like it would be rude. Did his age matter? Probably not, but she couldn't put it from her mind.

As they got back on the road, she wondered how she might work it into the conversation on the ride back. But the movement of the truck soon put her to sleep.

She woke to Jaylen gently shaking her shoulder. "Mel, we're home."

Blinking, she took in her surroundings, not quite sure where she was. The details of the vehicle's interior came into focus. Her cabin visible out the front window. Then, her brain put the pieces together.

They had taken a trip to the Olympic Center at Mel's request. She recalled the stench of the hockey rink, followed by the unsettling sensation of the giant ski jumps. Her cheeks warmed at the remembrance of Jaylen's arms around her as she cried her heart out.

She avoided looking at him in the driver seat next to her and stared out the window. The sky was darkening, the last faded rays of the sun peeking up above the silhouette of the trees behind the cabin.

"Where should I put the firewood?" he asked.

"Firewood?" she said stupidly. She had completely forgotten about her idea to search for firewood while on the road, but he hadn't.

"We passed an old bed and breakfast on the way home. There was a huge shed full of firewood, so I stopped. Put as much as I could fit in the back of the truck. I can do another round tomorrow if you want."

They exited the truck and she followed him around to the back of it. Stacks of wood filled the entire space underneath the raised solar panels in the bed of the truck.

"You did all this while I was sleeping?" She was

astounded she had slept through that.

He shrugged. "It wasn't a big deal. I backed the truck right up to the shed. It was just a matter of loading it in."

He must have been very quiet to not have woken Mel, who was a fairly light sleeper. Either that or she had been very worn out. She suspected it was actually a combination of both. Nevertheless, she was touched by his consideration of her.

"Where should I put it?" he asked again.

Mel knocked a knuckle on a piece of the wood. It was nicely seasoned but not rotting, so it was probably a type of wood that stayed green a long time, like oak. It also must have been stored in a nicely constructed wood shed to have stay in such great condition.

"I have a covered rack on the far side of the cabin. Though you can leave some on the porch for my indoor rack. I can help."

He shook his head. "No, I've got you. Take a look in the center console of the truck."

That piqued her interest. She headed to the cabin of the truck while Jaylen began stacking wood in his arms. She climbed back into the passenger seat and popped open the center console.

A bouquet of bright red roses greeted her. She counted as she pulled them out one-by-one. An even dozen.

The blooms were smaller and the petals less compact than the traditional ones that stores used to sell around Valentine's Day. There were no thorns on the stems to be wary of as she clutched them in her hands. On closer inspection, she saw the marks where the thorns had been removed. Yet more proof of Jaylen's thoughtfulness.

With steps that felt light for the first time that day, Mel practically danced to the side of the cabin where Jaylen was stacking wood on the covered rack.

"Thank you! They're perfect!" she practically shouted. "The roses, I mean."

He turned to her with that bright smile, his one dimple showing.

Before he could speak, Mel found herself rambling on. "I can dry the petals and use them in tea. Or, I can brew rose water and try it in a sweet cornbread for dessert. It could almost be like having cake. Do you think you'd like rose water cornbread?"

Jaylen's smiled quirked and his eyes glinted, like she'd accidentally told him a joke that she didn't understand but he did. "I like everything you cook."

She blushed, though she wasn't sure why. "Thanks. I'll get started on the rose water while I make dinner. Lentils tonight. Meet you on the porch in about an hour?"

"I'm looking forward to it."

He headed back to the truck to unload more wood. Mel watched him for a second before hurrying inside the cabin, excited for the possibilities of the roses.

CHAPTER 26

It was rare that Mel was gone from the cabin for a whole day. The turmoil from earlier had seemingly melted away during her nap on the ride home. With a smile, she set the roses on the kitchen counter and took a moment to take stock of what needed to be done to make dinner and prepare the rose water.

The fire had gone out in the wood stove, so she put more wood and tinder in it. She struck a match against the box, and with a satisfying *snick*, it lit up. She watched it burn for a few seconds, mesmerized by the miracle of fire.

One small strike and she could heat and sanitize water, cook a meal, or warm her home. She had flint and steel and, in theory, could light a fire with that, but she also had a very large supply of matches. As far as she could tell, they didn't go bad so long as they stayed dry. It was one of the things she had stocked up on when she could still do supply runs in the old truck.

She shook her head and quickly held the match to the tinder and dropped in into the stove before the flame could burn her fingers. In this moment, she was proud of her past self for the diligence and preparedness that allowed for an easy moment in the present. She needed a fire and she had the tools to easily do that. In a world that required total independence, that was something not to be taken for granted.

All of this was true, yet she couldn't totally shake the feeling that, at times, she took the vigilance too far to the point where worry took over any joy that was left in life. How could she find that balance?

She filled two pans with water, one for the lentils and one for the rose petals, and put them on the cook surface of the wood stove. She put more wood into the fire, hoping to speed up the heating process.

It was not lost on her that the convenience of running water and the abundance of firewood was due to Jaylen. She contemplated this while sprinkling the fresh rose petals in a pot of simmering water. She moved to chopping herbs and garlic for the lentils.

Having another person to share the load was a relief, especially when that person was Jaylen. Not only was he skilled in many ways that Mel wasn't, he was nice to be around. What would life be like if she had that all the time?

It reminded her that she had no idea what Jaylen's future plans were or what had brought him here in the first place. Come to think of it, Mel realized she knew very little about Jaylen's past.

Not that she had shared much about hers. She wasn't opposed to opening up more with him and hopefully learning more about him in return. They didn't even need to get into the heavy stuff; some of that was best left in the past. And maybe sharing with him might help her figure out what she wanted this situation.

She added the seasonings to the lentils and stirred the pot. She checked the rose water and found the petals had turned it a pretty pink color. The sweet scent of roses was filling up the cabin, making for a heady aroma. Her nose felt almost drunk with it.

She pulled that pot off the stove and set it aside to cool. As she removed the lid on the other pot to check the lentils, she got a savory whiff of the food that helped bring her out of the rose daze. She gave the lentils a stir and left them to cook longer.

Once the rose water was cool enough, she strained the liquid into a mason jar, adding a splash of vodka as a preservative. On a whim, she poured a shot's worth of vodka into each of two mugs to have with dinner.

Finally, she spooned a small portion of lentils out of the pot, blowing on it before tasting them. Not quite soft enough and little bland, she had to admit. She added a pinch of salt with a pang and replaced the lid. It was hard to use something that was in limited supply, but what was the point of having it if all she did was save it?

These were questions she hadn't thought much about in the last few years. As Jaylen said, she was a survivor, and that alone had kept her busy. But what if she could be something more?

Upon giving the lentils another stir, she could tell they were ready. She scooped the lentils into bowls, balanced everything on her large cutting board, and carried it out to the porch. Jaylen was waiting for her in one of the rocking chairs. The candles were lit, wood was stacked up neatly next to the front door, and his guitar was perched against the railing. He took a bowl and mug from the tray when she offered it to him with a "thanks."

"It's vodka," Mel explained. "In the mug. I used it in the rose water. I can get you water instead if you want."

She was suddenly worried that he was a recovering

alcoholic and that was why he had declined her offer of wine the other night. What if she was tempting him to fall off the wagon?

He contemplated the mug and shrugged. "It's a good night for a shot."

"You sure? I'm not trying to force you to drink or anything."

"Mel, it's okay. I used to like the occasional drink." He held up the mug. "Cheers!"

"Cheers," she said as they clinked cups.

They both downed the vodka. The initial burn of the alcohol settled into a warmth that relaxed Mel as they ate dinner.

With a slight ulterior motive of wanting to learn more about Jaylen, she racked her brain for a topic of conversation. Then, her gaze landed on the guitar.

"If you could see any band live, who would it be?" she asked.

"Oh." He seemed to be taken off-guard by the question but not displeased with it. He thought for a moment before saying, "Well, it's not really a band, though I guess he did have a band behind him. I'd have to say Jim Hendrix."

Mel shook her head thoughtfully as she chewed. She didn't know what kind of answer she had expected, but Jimi Hendrix made sense.

"What about you?" Jaylen asked.

She took another bite of food to give herself time to think. There were so many choices; she had quite forgotten the variety and scope of music in the before-times. She finally settled on one. "Queen."

"Queen?" He raised his eyebrows. "I wasn't expecting that."

"Can you imagine listening to Freddie Mercury singing

'Bohemian Rhapsody' live?"

"That would be something."

She tucked her legs up and sank deep into the rocking chair and let it slowly rock her into a deep state of relaxation. She wasn't tired—her nap had refreshed her energy—more content.

She pointed at the guitar. "Were you going to play tonight?"

He smiled that wide, bright smile that lit up his face. Heat rose in her chest, which she blamed on the vodka instead of on that smile. She shifted in her chair, hoping he didn't notice her reaction.

He simply picked up the guitar and strummed it softly. "I don't know how to play 'Bohemian Rhapsody,' but I think you'll like this one."

Mel quickly recognized the song as he began a rendition of "Mad World." She didn't know all the words and couldn't remember who the artist was, but she hummed along at the chorus. Jaylen's resonate voice brought tears to her eyes.

When he finished, he launched right into "Wish You Were Here" by Pink Floyd. She imagined the birds settling down for the night, being serenaded by the beautiful music. His next song was "Ain't No Sunshine," another one where she couldn't remember the artist's name.

She could probably find some way to look it up, but so much knowledge was lost or hard to access with Mel as the only living steward of all of humanity. Jaylen's form on her porch and his music carrying into the night was proof that this was no longer true. There were two of them now, and that was double the living knowledge than Mel had previously thought existed.

Jaylen played into the night as he treated her to an eclectic and somewhat melancholic concert. It felt like gaining insight into his life, even if he wasn't sharing specific details. Mel secretly thought that it was better than any Queen concert.

CHAPTER 27

As the spring season progressed, Mel focused on getting organized in the garden. It was a critical time for her staple crops like lentils, corn, potatoes, and sunflowers. There were also the fresh food crops that were plentiful in the growing season and were harder to store for winter, things like tomatoes, peppers, various greens, and cucumbers. Not broccoli, though...never broccoli.

With a pencil tucked behind her ear and a small notebook in the back pocket of her jeans, she headed out to the garden. She monitored how much of each crop was growing, calculating if she had enough plants to produce food to last through the winter. She also took into account possible crop loss from insects, weather, or other unfavorable conditions.

A full watering can stood at one end of a row of lentils. Not enough time had passed since the water pump trauma for her to take easy access to water for granted. After fixing the wiring problem, Jaylen had given the whole water pump system a thorough check. He'd deemed it in good shape, and barring any disasters, said it should last her a good long while.

Since then, Jaylen seemed content to stick around, but she wondered how long that would last. He hadn't hung out around the cabin much during the last few days, and she wondered what he had been up to.

They had fallen into a kind of pattern. As the sun would draw closer to the horizon, Jaylen would turn up on her porch and they'd share dinner. At first, she had provided most of the food, but he had begun bringing his own assortment of provisions along.

There were things foraged from the forest around them, like mushrooms and berries. He was far better at foraging than Mel had ever been. She was always too nervous she'd misidentify a plant and end up poisoning herself, but she trusted his knowledge of the forest.

He even hunted and prepared a goose over an outdoor fire one night. Mel had never gotten a taste for goose jerky, but she found herself enjoying the freshly cooked bird. She had shared some of her pickling juice with Jaylen for a marinade, and it toned down the gaminess while adding extra moistness to the meat.

They'd spend each evening together until Mel retired to the cabin and Jaylen headed off to sleep in his truck. It was hard not to get used to having him around, even while she waited for him to announce he was leaving. Metaphors about skating on thin ice came to mind, but she was having too much fun to worry about falling through to the icy waters.

The thing was, she liked cooking for someone other than herself. She liked having another person to share meals with. And she really liked that the other person was Jaylen.

She blew her hair out of her face in frustration as she recorded numbers in her notebook, trying not to be distracted by this man who was both a savior and a mystery. And damn good company with his musical talents and swoon-worthy smile.

Aside from preparing herself for him leaving, one of the reasons she wanted to find out about Jaylen's future plans was to figure out if she needed to grow extra crops to account for him staying through the winter. She would have to plant them soon.

Though, as she looked over what she had already planted, there was enough to go around so long as the plants continued to flourish. She walked to the north of the property to an area near the woods where only wild grasses were growing. She could clear out the grasses and fertilize the dirt with soil from her compost pile.

Not that Jaylen would necessarily plan on relying on her if he did stay. He clearly could take care of himself.

She pondered the workload of a new garden area versus the act of simply asking Jaylen what he planned to do. As she saw it, the extra work would probably be easier than initiating the dreaded conversation. And extra crops were never a bad thing.

She was probably overthinking and overplanning again. It was dangerous territory to think in anything long-term when it came to another person. It was harder than she had ever imagined to think about letting someone in again after losing everything and everyone she'd ever loved. And what if she was just a temporary distraction for him?

She should really just talk to him, she told herself as she headed to the chicken coop. She examined a cracked fence post that would probably need to be replaced. Rachel Lynde came strutting over to see what Mel was doing and pecked at the post.

"Nothing to see here," she said in a sing-song voice to the chicken. "Or to eat. You've already had your meal for the day."

The post was made of fresher wood than the others that had faded to gray over time. It was the ones he had replaced earlier in the year when it had cracked. She shouldn't have had to replace it so soon, unless she had done something wrong when she had installed it.

She ran her hand over the crack and gasped when a splinter dug into the skin of her palm. The shard of wood was easy enough to pick out, and she flicked it away.

Building things was not her strong suit, not like Jaylen. His work would have lasted longer than six months, she was sure of that.

She groaned that she couldn't get him out of her head. Did he even have a plan for the future? Without any real evidence to support her hunch, she got the feeling he had been living a nomadic life and didn't really make plans. And if he were to make plans, did she want them to include her?

Jaylen was a force that had disrupted her simple life at the cabin, but he was also someone who brought joy to her life. She'd been enjoying his company, even as some part of her kept him at arm's length. She didn't want to fall for someone who would leave her.

Besides, she wasn't even sure she was falling for him. It was more likely that her feelings stemmed from the fact that he was literally the only other person in the world. A crush of convenience and proximity, rather than one of meaningful connection.

The more she thought about the whole situation, the more complicated it became. Until she had no more answers as to what to do than she did before and began overthinking the whole thing. It was a circle of futile thoughts.

She grumbled and kicked at the broken post, snapping it in half. The top half hung at an angle from the chicken wire, while the bottom half remained stuck in the dirt.

Rachel Lynde clucked at her in dismay. Mel was about to yell at the chicken but decided not to take her anger out on the innocent bird.

She walked toward the wooded area at the back of the property, stopping at the tree line. Resting her hands on her knees, she bent forward and closed her eyes. She took slow, steady breaths until her temper calmed.

Mel was about to open her eyes when she heard the click of a gun cocking, a sound she only knew from movies she'd seen long ago but one that was unmistakable all the same.

She stood tall and whipped around to find Jaylen standing about ten feet away, gun pointed right at her.

"Don't move," he said in a deadly quiet voice.

Chapter 28

Here Mel had been contemplating how this man might fit into her future, and now Jaylen was pointing a shotgun at her. Staring at his finger poised on the trigger, Mel's first instinct was to raise her hands in the air like she was the bad guy in an action movie. But Jaylen had said not to move.

She stayed frozen in place. If her mind had been moving in frustrated circles a few minutes ago, now it moved at a frantic pace, darting across many thoughts at once. All of them leading to one question that she couldn't figure out an answer to. Why would Jaylen be holding her at gun point?

His gaze was intensely focused, his lips carving a harsh line across his face. Looking into those brown eyes that were usually so soft and caring, but were now hard and serious, Mel saw a stranger. Maybe she had never really known him.

"Don't take your eyes off me," he said with that same deadly voice. "Very slowly, walk toward me."

She replayed the last few seconds of life in her head. She stared at his face and questioned what that hard expression meant. Could she be seeing something other than cold violence there? Despite how little she knew about his past or future intentions, she had grown to trust him.

She put that trust to the test and took one slow step toward him. Then, another and another, until she was mere inches from the gun. This close to the weapon, it was clear it was not aimed at her but at some point above her left shoulder.

Mel's chest rose rapidly up and down with her shallow breathing. This close to him, she saw lines etched across his forehead and beads of sweat forming at his hairline. Now she recognized this expression. It was the same one he had given her when she'd fallen off her bike and when she'd been shaken by the looming stillness of the ski jumps.

It was concern on his face, definitely concern.

This was only confirmed all the more when a kind of shuffling noise came from behind her, followed by a snort.

She gasped. Was there another survivor in the world that had somehow found them? A person, hardened in their efforts to survive, who now posed a threat to Mel and Jaylen.

Beneath the fear was relief. He did care about her after all.

"Look at me, Mel," Jaylen said, his voice still a harsh rumble, but there was a slight waver of fear there as well. "Stay still."

She blinked twice in agreement, and he seemed to understand as he nodded almost imperceptibly.

He adjusted his grip on the shotgun. Very slowly, he took one step to the side so he was no longer face-to-face with her. With incremental maneuvers, he effectively put himself in between Mel and whatever threat was behind her.

Fighting against every urge that was screaming at her to turn around, she did as he had told and stayed still.

All that discipline was all for nothing when Jaylen shouted, "Go away!"

She spun around quickly to find him waving the gun

above his head wildly. Beyond him, right at the tree line where Mel had been standing moments ago, was a black bear. It was leaner than she thought a bear should be, and its fur was matted and dirty.

The bear lowered its muzzle and stared them down. It lunged upwards with its front paws before slamming them on the ground and letting out a huff of air. The ground shook on impact, and Mel involuntarily took a step back.

Keeping one hand on the gun, Jaylen reached behind his back for her in a protective gesture.

"Don't run," he said, clearly to her, not the bear.

She nodded in return, though he didn't see her as his attention was fixed on the animal. Mel's chest was heaving as if she had run several miles uphill. She sucked in enough air to say a breathy "okay."

He returned both hands to the gun and shouldered the weapon, poised to shoot. Stomping his feet and yelling, not so much words this time but his own growly noise, Jaylen attempted to scare the bear away. The bear only huffed at them.

Then, it lumbered closer. Jaylen tightened his grip on the gun and pulled the trigger.

The shot was so loud, Mel reflexively closed her eyes. She didn't see what happened next, but she felt an arm wrap around her.

She quickly opened her eyes to see nothing but the back of his plaid shirt, the gun still in one hand but lowered at his side. The other arm kept a tight grip on her. She peeked around him to catch of glimpse of the bear running off into the woods.

Once it was out of sight, Jaylen turned to her and asked, "Are you okay?"

It was the first thing he had ever said to her and ever

since then, it seemed like he was constantly asking her if she was okay.

The truth was that she hadn't been okay for a very long time. Five years ago, she had been sick and grieving. When she had resolved to live all on her own, she thought she had been okay, but the loneliness never left. She hadn't realized how bone-achingly deep the loneliness was until Jaylen had shown up.

So, no, she wasn't okay. She also knew that's not what he really meant by the question, not this time anyway.

"I'm not hurt," she answered truthfully.

Jaylen leaned down and carefully set the gun on the ground, his gaze never leaving her face. He stood before her, his hands gently caressing her arms. She hadn't quite caught her breath, and the way he was looking at her with such heat in his eyes wasn't helping matters.

His chest also rose and fell heavily with labored breathing. He pulled her into his chest and crushed her into a hug. Her face pressed against his shirt buttons.

"We're okay, we're okay," he said into her hair.

A lump rose in her throat as she wrapped her arms around him, the warmth of his body spreading through her. She breathed in his scent, a mix of earthiness and sweat with a hint of minty freshness reminiscent of aftershave. Though she had no idea where he would've gotten aftershave.

Once she pushed that thought away, she was completely overwhelmed with his closeness. His arms around her. His body pressed against hers. His lips in her hair.

He pulled away too soon. She groaned with displeasure until she caught his smoldering gaze, not on her eyes this time but her lips.

"Mel," he whispered.

She stood on her tiptoes and parted her lips without any

intention of speaking. He took the cue and lowered his mouth, barely brushing his lips against hers. They were a little rough, but smooth lips were a luxury left in the past. It was easy to ignore the roughness with the other sensations that lit up inside her at the contact.

She stretched farther up on her toes to deepen the kiss. He leaned down even more. The kiss was long and tender, but it still ended too soon for Mel's liking.

Jaylen stared at her, eyes glazed and heated, an unspoken question between them about how far they wanted this to go. She answered by taking his hand and leading him to the porch.

At the door to the cabin, she turned, biting her lip. "Do you want to come in?"

He nodded. She swung open the door, and Jaylen entered her home for the first time.

CHAPTER 29

Late that night, Mel and Jaylen lay in her bed, the one she had slept in more times alone than with her late husband. They talked of things that were too painful to speak of in the light of day. Topics that were reserved for a time when only a hint of moonlight provided just enough light with which to see each other.

When the world was quiet. When their minds were dull with fatigue and their hearts soft with near sleep. That was the time for topics best saved for the liminal state between waking and dreaming.

Mel had told Jaylen of her hysterectomy and inability to get pregnant when they'd first entered the cabin because it was a pressing matter at the time. Now, as her cheek rested against his bare chest, they spoke in hushed whispers of those they had lost that were most dear to them.

For Mel, that was Daniel and their dog Bruno, her parents, and the many children she had taught over the years. For Jaylen, that was his fiancé Nikki, a younger sister, and his mother.

She told him how Daniel had loved hockey, not mentioning that it was one of the reasons for visiting the

Olympic Center. He paused in his affectionate caresses of her hair when she mentioned this, so she figured he was putting the pieces together.

He told her how Nikki had a beautiful singing voice. How he had never been much for going to church after his mom stopped making him go, but he showed up every week to listen to Nikki sing in the choir. She had a persnickety—Jaylen's word—cat named Butter that took a long time to get used to him when he moved in with Nikki. Eventually, though, Butter would curl up on his lap when they would watch movies, almost seeming to prefer it to Nikki's.

"She would always look over at me and Butter and smile," he said. "So I knew she wasn't jealous. Nikki wasn't the jealous type."

In turn, Mel spoke of Bruno. How she and Daniel had gotten him as a puppy when they bought their house. He had been so energetic, they had to keep all the breakables in the spare bedroom with the door shut.

"He was old in the end," she whispered. "But he probably had a few good years left in him."

Jaylen kissed her forehead as she fell silent. Her eyelids had grown heavy with fatigue, but the rest of her felt lighter for having confided in Jaylen. For having this man to talk to. For having a friend after so many years of solitude.

She thought about how she was falling in love with him, but was too sleepy to worry too much about it. She fell asleep to the steady rise and fall of Jaylen's chest beneath her.

Mel woke to the rooster's call early the next morning, her limbs tangled in Jaylen's. His body was warm against her back, and a hint of sunlight came in through the window near the bed. After an initial burst of happiness at her present situation, her self-consciousness kicked in.

Anxious to face him, she feigned sleep until she felt him slip out of bed. Only then, did she open her eyes and roll over.

"Good morning, ma'am." He stood next to the bed and offered her that smile of his.

That was all it took for her to dispel any notion that she needed to be embarrassed. She stayed in bed while he dressed, snuggling deep into the blankets where it was warm.

Jaylen found the firewood stacked in a corner and stoked the wood stove like he belonged there in the cabin. Like he had been doing it every morning for years. She bit back a smile as she got dressed.

"Can I make you tea?" she asked. Mr. Coffee Drinker shot her an incredulous look. "It's good. I promise."

"Goose jerky, good?"

Mel snorted. "No. For real good."

He threw his hands up in defeat. "Alright, I trust you. I'll have some tea."

She clapped her hands in excitement.

He placed a hand on her cheek and kissed her on the head. "I'm gonna take a look at that broken fence post in the chicken coop."

"I'll bring your tea out when it's ready."

Once Jaylen left, she attempted to tame her hair into a bun. She took a moment to appreciate how easy it was to fill the kettle with enough water for two teas. Then, she went about combining the best ingredients she could find for a former coffee addict who she hoped to convert into a tea drinker.

Taking stock of the fresh herbs she had growing on the porch, she quickly disregarded most of them. Peppermint and lemon balm were two of her favorites, but they felt too bright for Jaylen's palette. The earthy tones of rosemary and tarragon might do the trick. She snipped off a couple of sprigs of each, plus some lemon balm for herself, and returned inside.

She roll the rosemary between her palms to release the flavor and popped the herbs into the tea strainer. Retreating to her pantry, she decided against chamomile—too sleepy. Her gaze landed on a small jar of dried anise seed. It had a licorice flavor that wasn't her favorite but was good for congestion, so she kept it around to treat colds. A pinch of anise was added to the strainer.

It was a good start, but she felt like she needed one more thing to tie the flavors together. She thought back to the jalapeno omelets she and Jaylen had the night he first played guitar. He liked spicy food, so maybe he would like his tea spicy, too.

She fetched the last jar of pickled jalapenos from the pantry. There were only two peppers left, but there was a bunch of seeds floating in the pickle juice. She caught three with a spoon and rinsed them, careful not to lose them down the sink. Hopefully, that would get rid of the vinegar flavor.

Mel poured the boiling water over the ingredients in the tea strainers. She let them steep for a few minutes while she scooped leftover lentils into two bowls. She put the mugs and bowls on a tray, slipped an empty basket over her wrist, and carried everything outside to the Adirondack chairs.

She left the teas on the arms of the chairs and went to the chicken coop where Jaylen was working on getting the old post out of the ground. She dumped the smaller bowl of lentils into Gilbert's pen and let herself into the chicken coop where she fed the chickens and collected their eggs in her basket.

When she was done, she and Jaylen went and sat in the

chairs. She handed him his mug, and he sniffed at the tea.

"Take a sip," she encouraged him.

He blew on it. "Too hot."

Mel pointedly took a sip of her tea. Definitely not too hot. Out of the corner of her eyes, she watched Jaylen raise the mug to his mouth and drink in the tea.

He coughed, spluttered really.

"That bad?" she asked.

"No," he said, his watering eyes telling a different story. "Hot!"

Mel took another sip of the tea to confirm it was not too hot. "I don't know what you're talking about. It's the perfect temperature."

"Not the temperature." He coughed. "Hot as in spicy."

"Ah. That would be the jalapeno seeds."

"You put jalapeno seeds in my tea!" Jaylen sniffed at the mug again.

She shrugged. "You like strong coffee and spicy food."

"Spicy food, not beverages."

Trying not to laugh, she offered him her mug. "Here, try mine."

They switched, Jaylen eyeing the new tea suspiciously.

"There's no jalapeno in that one," she reassured him.

He cautiously brought it to his lips and took the tiniest taste Mel had ever seen. His eyes widened. He took a bigger swig.

"Not bad," he said. "Lemony."

He offered it back to her, but she shook him off.

"No, you finish that one."

She decided to try the concoction she had made for him and regretted it the instant the liquid hit her tongue. She spat it onto the ground. Despite barely having gotten any of it in her mouth, a burning sensation went down her throat and up into her nose.

"Oh, dear," she said.

"It's a sinus clearer, for sure."

Jaylen laughed and downed the rest of the lemon balm tea. He seemed to be enjoying it, and Mel sincerely hoped he would stick around long enough for her to convert him into a tea drinker.

Chapter 30

Mel went ahead and cleared the wild grasses from the northern section of the yard for a new garden. She hauled many loads of dark soil from the oldest compost pile and mixed it in with native dirt. There she planted sunflowers, potatoes, and corn. Extra food was always a good thing, regardless of how long Jaylen ended up staying. And he seemed content to stay at least a little while longer.

That night, Mel was tired after a long day in the garden when Jaylen started listing out the improvements he wanted to make on the property—with her permission, of course. Top of the list was fixing up the chicken coops and adding fencing around the compost piles. Both areas that might attract a hungry bear.

The dying light from the stove just reached Jaylen's face as he lay next to her. He tucked an errant curl behind her ear and kissed her forehead.

"I want to make sure you're safe," he said.

In her mind, there was an unspoken part about him wanting her to stay safe once he left. She tried not to dwell on that and instead cherished their time together.

Time and time again, she had chickened out on asking

him about his future plans, until she finally had to admit she was never going to ask. It didn't stop the growing problem that each night she spent with him further pushed her into wanting him to stay forever.

Jaylen, who was blissfully unaware of the turmoil inside Mel, talked on. "I can't believe there was a bear in your yard. I thought I'd never see one again. I wonder what other random mammals are out there."

"So long as the squirrels stay away from my tomatoes," she said sleepily. "They used to pick them when they were green, take one bite, and discard them. That was back at the old house when I only had a few plants. Daniel used to find me holding a rotting green tomato, cursing at the oak tree in the yard."

The bed shook beneath them with Jaylen's laughter. "I can picture it."

"I can't," she whispered, a sober realization dawning on her.

"Can't what?"

"Picture it. Daniel's face. I can't picture his face." She turned toward the wall and kind of closed in on herself as tears began to fall. "I didn't take any pictures up here with me. I thought I was coming here to die."

Jaylen snuggled closer and spooned her, caressing her hair. He comforted her without saying anything. What was there to say? They both knew words could not soothe the deep grief they both felt.

She was almost asleep when he whispered, "I want to build you a solar car of your own. Would you want that?"

She mumbled, "Mmmhmm."

She wanted to tell him no, she didn't want her own car. She'd rather Jaylen and his truck stay with her. But if that was what he wanted to do, then she wouldn't stop him. Every new item for his list meant him sticking around longer.

Jaylen spent the next few days raiding her shed for supplies. In there, he found chicken wire, a few spare posts, shovels, and a full box of hand tools. He made a long list for the hardware store that included galvanized fence wire, lumber, concrete mix, buckets, and a post hole digger, which Mel hadn't even known was a thing. She had dug all the holes for the chicken coops with a shovel.

She had also been composting her yard scraps and food waste together, but Jaylen proposed two different systems. One system would be an open fencing for yard waste. The other would be a closed system for food waste. He told her was hoping he could find composting bins for the latter, again so as not to attract any creatures, bears or otherwise. She didn't really understand all the intricacies but trusted him to do a good job.

The fence work was long, sweaty work that kept Jaylen busy for days. While he did all that, Mel worked in the garden. It was a busy time of year for gardening.

On one particularly hot afternoon when she was hungry, sweaty, and tired, she reminded herself she would have plenty of time to rest in the winter. Those cold, short days would have her mostly housebound and itching to get back out in the sunshine. But now was a time for work to keep her belly full this winter.

Mel tried to stick to two meals a day and snacks as necessary because it was more economical to eat that way, and it kept her from having to stoke up the wood stove all day long, which kept the house cooler this time of year.

When she couldn't take the sun anymore, she went inside for a glass of water and a snack. Here, she was able to strip down to a tank top and underwear without worrying about sunburn. She stood in front of the open window at the back of the cabin where a slight breeze was coming in and munched on a handful of raisins. From there, she could watch Jaylen working on the fence. She admired his strong muscles, shiny with sweat, as he mixed concrete and water in a big bucket.

She put her pants back on and brought a wet washcloth and some water outside for him. He drank the entire glass of water in one long chug.

"Thanks, ma'am," he said as he handed the glass back to her.

She no longer rolled her eyes at the "ma'am" joke. It was a gem she tucked away in her memory to pull out one day like a lost treasure.

"Will you be able to take tomorrow off from the fence?" she asked.

He looked around at the materials spread all around. "Yeah. It'll give the posts time to fully set up. Why?"

"It's strawberry season. I usually take my bike out to this strawberry patch that's not too far from here, but getting enough berries home in one piece can be a bit tricky. I usually do more than one trip. If we take your truck, we can do it all in one day."

"Sounds yummy."

She leaned toward him for a kiss, and he bent down and obliged.

"I'll make you strawberry pancakes for your trouble," she said.

He caressed her face. "It's no trouble. It's my pleasure."

Mel felt the blush go right to the tips of her ears as he kissed her deeper and then strayed to her neck. She was probably the color of a strawberry right now.

Yes, she thought, I'll keep this man as long as I can.

CHAPTER 31

Strawberries ripened around the same time each year, but it could be notoriously difficult to pinpoint an exact date for such an outing, even with Mel's meticulous records of past seasons. There was one year where she had ridden her bike all the way out to the strawberry fields that had once housed a pick-your-own farm, only to discover she had missed the season altogether. It was a few rotting berries among a field of plants picked clean of fruit. She'd cried almost the entire way home for her efforts having gone to waste.

Today, Mel was confident they would be successful. And with Jaylen's truck available, the timing was less critical. They could easily come back if they showed up too early, though there was nothing to be done about coming too late. She hoped they weren't too late this year.

Jaylen was waiting in the passenger seat when she met him at his truck. She opened the driver's door and poked her head inside. "What are you doing?"

His face broke into that heart-melting smile, his dimple winking at her. "I thought you should drive today. Good practice for when you have your own truck."

Feeling her mood dampen, she shoved the basket of

water and food at Jaylen and placed several cardboard boxes and her straw hat in the back seat. "You know I'm a fully licensed driver."

"I know, and I have the utmost confidence in your driving abilities, but this truck drives a little different than what you're used to...ma'am."

She climbed into the driver's seat with a grumble and hit the start button.

"It pretty much works the same as any automatic car," he explained. "Think old-school because I haven't enabled the technology package like the back-up camera. That's to maximize the battery life. The big thing to be aware of is your speed. Anything above thirty-five miles per hour is going to run the battery down too fast and we risk having to stop and let it recharge."

"Got it. No lead foot." She put the truck in drive and slowly drove out of the driveway onto the road.

"How about air conditioning?" she asked cheekily. "It's a little hot out today."

"Very funny." He rolled his eyes and cracked open his window.

Mel opened her own window about halfway, enjoying the way the wind blew in her face enough to feel it but not so hard as to make a complete mess of her hair. Even with the speed restrictions, she couldn't believe how much faster the ride was compared to when she did it on her bike.

It felt like hardly any time before she was pulling into the dirt parking lot at the bottom of the hill where the strawberry fields sat. She had almost missed the turnoff because it was so overgrown with weeds. Luckily, the brush blocking the entrance was all small stuff that the truck could easily drive over.

Mel popped the straw hat on her head, and the pair

trudged up the hill with the cardboard boxes. Before they even reached the rows of strawberry plants, Mel spied red fruit peeking out from underneath the green leaves. She blew out a sigh of relief that turned to astonishment when she got a closer look at the strawberries.

They were ripe and fat and plentiful. A bumper crop, for sure. With two people picking and no need to restrict herself to what she could get home with on the bike, Mel practically danced with excitement over all the strawberry jam she'd be able to make.

Her knees crunched in protest as she squatted down and showed Jaylen how to look under the leaves to find the bunches of strawberries. She twisted one off in demonstration, keeping a small bit of stem attached.

She bit into the sun-warmed fruit and moaned. It was juicy and sweet, a perfect bite. Jaylen wet his lips and stared at her while she finished off the strawberry on the second bite. She tossed the stem aside.

"You have to try one." She bent to pick another. When she stood, a ripe strawberry in hand, he was waiting patiently, his mouth open in anticipation. She plucked the stem and leaves off and popped the whole strawberry into his mouth.

His eyes widened as he slowly chewed. How did this man make eating a strawberry look so sexy?

"Oh, wow," he said when he finished. "Can I have another?"

Mel retrieved a third strawberry. This time when she stood, Jaylen had moved closer. He didn't wait for her to remove the stem but guided her hand directly to his lips before taking the whole fruit into his mouth.

Heart in throat, she watched him close his eyes and chew. Without opening his eyes, he clutched her waist and pressed his lips to hers. Her hat fell off, but she didn't care. He was heat and sweetness, the strawberry flavor lingering on his tongue when it entered her mouth.

They stayed wrapped up in each other under the sun, neither of them having their fill when they pulled apart. Despite how close they had grown over the last few weeks, sharing a bed each night, Mel wondered if the overwhelming way this man disarmed her would ever fade.

She cleared her throat. "I guess we should get started."

Jaylen nodded, the want Mel felt mirrored in his expression.

Reluctantly, she moved to the row of plants next to him and focused on the task at hand. They filled the boxes in no time, leaving behind so many ripe strawberries. The birds and bugs would enjoy them, and the leftover ones would fall and rot, feeding the soil.

"Should we come back tomorrow and pick more?" Jaylen asked as they each carried a box down the hill.

"I don't think I can spare that many canning jars just for strawberry jam," Mel admitted. "I'll need some for blueberry jam. And I don't want to use up too many of the sealing lids. I only have a limited supply of those." She bit her lip. "I don't know what I'll do when I run out."

They headed back up the hill for the remaining boxes of fruit.

"I'll add it to my list of things to keep an eye out for," he said. "When we get home, you can show me what they look like."

He said home like it was his home, not just Mel's. She was afraid to admit how much she hoped it would be their home forever.

CHAPTER 32

Summer was probably Mel's busiest time of year. There were crops to gather and process and then more planting to make the most of the fall harvest. When she wasn't working outside, Mel prepped for winter with canning, drying, and pickling the bounty of the garden. Her pantry was now restocked with dried strawberries and jam and would continue to fill up as the season went on.

It was the opposite of her time as a teacher when summer was slow, a time to recharge after a long school year. That way she could give her best to the next set of students in the fall. It was one of the reasons Mel and her husband had decided to buy the cabin. They both loved to ski in the winter, but the cabin was also a place they could go in the summer to relax and recharge. They'd had plans to check out the antique stores, swim in the lake, hike, and visit a local vineyard.

Their one summer with the cabin in the before-times, Mel had spent most of her time cleaning and decorating it. Daniel had only come up once to help supervise the installation of the water pump. None of their plans had come to fruition. Since then, the cabin had become Mel's lifeline, but it was also a place of hard work.

This summer, she found the work easier to bear with Jaylen nearby. Once he finished mending the existing chicken coops, he built a new one for breeding them. In the book on the topic, Mel had learned that there were many different characteristics to look for when considering which hen to place with a rooster. This information had narrowed the choices down to Marilla and Anne Shirley as possible mates for Gilbert. As a fan of the books, she planned to go with the obvious choice of Anne Shirley.

After a thorough inspection of the cabin, Jaylen found more tasks, like replacing a rotted board on the porch and fixing a couple of loose shingles on the roof. He also made rain barrels to store water for the plants. Occasionally, he would take a drive in search for an electric truck that he could convert to solar-powered for Mel, but he'd had no luck in finding one yet. For her part, she was in no hurry for that to happen.

Jaylen was almost done with his latest project, which was digging out a root cellar for long-term food storage. This was particularly useful this year when Mel had planted all those extra potatoes and lentils. It was the second-to-last item on his list. The dreaded solar-powered truck for Mel was last on the list. Finding the right kind of vehicle was proving difficult, much to her delight.

Today, Jaylen had headed to the hardware store to get the last few supplies for the root cellar and hadn't yet returned. She was so distracted thinking about him that she had forgotten to grab her gloves for weeding. She threw herself into the chore and instantly regretted it when she tugged at a particularly stubborn weed and a thorn pierced her palm.

"Ow!" she yelled, startling the birds out of a nearby tree.

She grumbled the whole way to the shed where she retrieved her gloves. Weeding took up the rest of her day.

Mel was making dinner, windows all open to let in the fresh air while the wood stove was going, when she heard Jaylen come home. The truck itself was quiet, but the tires on the dirt driveway were not. She looked out the front window to find the sky was turning a light pink.

Jaylen hopped out of the truck, a big self-satisfied grin on his face. Her heart sank. Before he even said it, Mel knew what was coming.

"Look what I found," he announced when he came inside and handed her a paper bag.

In her distracted state, she hadn't noticed him carrying it. She peeked inside to find boxes of canning lids in various sizes.

"I drove by a big general store and decided to see what they had," he said. "There were canning jars, too, if you need them. I knew you needed the lids, but I wasn't sure about the jars. I'll be heading back that way tomorrow if you want me to get them."

"Sure. Thank you."

She leaned up and kissed him on the cheek. She was afraid to ask why he'd be heading back there tomorrow, but he had an answer.

"The store is really close to something else I found today."

Mel blinked, her eyes suddenly watery, as she went back to chopping vegetables. "Oh yeah."

"A truck!" he said triumphantly. "I found a truck for you."

And there it was, the thing she'd been dreading. She paused in her chopping, but Jaylen didn't seem to notice as he talked on.

"It's in great condition, except I couldn't get it started to bring it here. It's probably better if I work on it there anyway because it's in a garage. It's only about two hours away."

Abruptly, she turned and hugged him, burying her face in his chest.

"Thank you," she mumbled into his shirt. She wasn't even sure what she was thanking him for because it certainly wasn't about the truck. Maybe she was just feeling grateful that he was here and she could hug him like this.

He stroked her hair. "Of course. Anything for you."

Just as quickly as she had decided to hug him, she went back to making dinner. Jaylen washed up, and they met up at the porch.

Her hands shook a little as she brought the plates out. She had prepared a salad bursting with fresh greens, tomatoes, cucumbers, and radishes, topped with slices of hard-boiled eggs. She didn't normally drink tea with dinner in the summertime, but she found comfort in the warm mug in her hands and was glad she had strayed from the norm tonight.

Jaylen thanked her and gestured at the mug. "That smells good."

She mustered a smile. "It's lavender and chamomile. Would you like me to make you one?"

He actually thought about it a moment before saying, "No. Not tonight. But I'll take one in the morning."

Her grin grew in her triumph over having converted him to a tea drinker. That quickly faded as he excitedly talked about the truck.

"It's the same make and model as mine, only a year older. I've already scouted out where I can get the solar panels. It'll take a couple of trips with my truck, but I should be able to get all the materials in place in a few days. And unless there are complications, another day or two of work should have it up and running."

She glanced up from her plate and gave him another smile, feigning excitement over his plans. But she was thinking about *her* plans…all the plans she'd had for them that they probably wouldn't get to do now.

Blueberry season was coming up. They'd had such fun picking strawberries that she had been excited for blueberry picking and making jam, especially now that she had more canning lids. He also wouldn't be around to see the big sunflower field bloom when the flowers often grew bigger than Mel's head. Or to go apple picking in the fall, or for pumpkin season, or to see the first snowfall. Despite her efforts not to make future plans for the two of them, it seemed her subconscious had been doing it all along.

A few days to gather materials and a couple more to retrofit the truck with solar panels. Was that all the time she had left with Jaylen?

"Mel?" he asked, breaking her from her thoughts. "You okay?"

She realized she was clutching the tea mug in her hands tightly, her salad left untouched.

"Yeah," she said. "Just tired."

Now that she said it, she felt how true that was. A bone-deep tiredness had settled over her, one she was all too familiar with. The kind of tired she'd hoped to never experience again. But one she feared was on her way if Jaylen truly left her.

CHAPTER 33

All the next day, Mel was jittery with nerves with the world taking on a dreamlike quality. Her mind kept drifting to Jaylen, who had left early to work on the truck. She imagined him hooking up the solar panels and firing up the truck. But instead of driving back to the cabin, he rolled down the windows, laughed manically, and sped away down the highway.

She couldn't shake the tiredness from her body as she finished her chores and listlessly made dinner. If Jaylen noticed how quiet she was while they ate, he didn't mention it. If she had been paying better attention to him, she might have read something into the fact that he was equally as quiet, his forehead occasionally wrinkling in concern when he stole a look at her.

When Mel and Jaylen were tucked in bed, one of his big arms draped across her midsection and the crickets chirping outside the open window, she was finally able to get out the words she'd been holding back for a long time.

"Jaylen," she began, her quiet voice shaking on his name. She inhaled deeply and let it out slowly. His hand found hers under the blanket and he gently held it.

"What is it?" he whispered.

It had always been easier at night in the dark to talk about the hard things, but this one was maybe too hard. In her mind, she told herself that she could do this and took another deep breath.

"I need to know when you're—" her voice broke. She dove in and finally just said it, "I need to know when you're going to leave me."

As soon as the words landed, it was as if time stopped. Jaylen's whole body stilled, his arm stiff around her, and his breathing seemed to cease. Even the steady chirp of the crickets fell into a muted, distant noise.

As the world paused, Mel also stiffened, her heart stuttering in her chest.

Finally, Jaylen rolled away from her, the warm cocoon of him gone. Time resumed and the world rushed back in. Mel's body went limp. She kept her back to him as their heavy breaths filled the room and the outside sounds returned.

"Mel, I—" he cut himself off and let out a kind of moan. "I—"

This time she cut him off. "It's fine. You don't owe me anything. I probably owe you for all you've done around here. You've always been free to leave whenever you want to."

The mattress bounced as he rolled back toward her and touched her shoulder. "Mel, it's not that I want to leave you. It's just...it's just there are others relying on me."

She sat up and faced him. "Others?"

He groaned and also sat up.

"Jaylen, what do you mean. What others?"

When he didn't answer right away, she sank back down on the bed and stared at the ceiling. She couldn't look at him. How could he drop a bomb like that and not explain himself?

"I've been trying to tell you for..." he paused. "Well, pretty much since I got here."

She could hear the regret in his voice, but she wasn't sure what he was regretting. Not telling her sooner? Staying too long? Staying at all?

She chanced a glance at him and found he was rubbing his beard.

"What have you been trying to tell me?" she said with a sharp edge to each word.

"We're not the only ones who survived!"

Mel blinked back tears as a headache mounted at her temples. Her vision blurred, and before she could say anything, Jaylen was talking again.

"I come from a small community of survivors back in D.C. Most of us lived and worked there before the pandemic. Miguel, a buddy of mine from the Army—an unbelievably smart guy—he worked for a pharmaceutical company in Maryland. He was working on a vaccine, a universal one that could work against all viruses."

Her vision cleared and she stared at his earnest face, a few fine lines on his forehead she had never noticed before. She listened to him without thinking about what he was saying. This way it was like he was telling a story—a fictional one—not the truth of what he'd been keeping from her all this time.

"Right before things got bad, he called me and told me to come in and get a vaccine. He said it wasn't approved yet, but he was worried, very worried, about the chatter he was hearing from other parts of the world where the virus was already spreading."

He paused and wiped a tear from his cheek. His Adam's apple bobbed up and down as he swallowed heavily. When he next spoke, his words were thick with emotion.

"I was skeptical. It all sounded like hardcore conspiracy theory shit. But, Miguel, man, he was the smartest guy I ever met. Too smart to ignore. I drove out and met him at his house. He never even invited me in and wore a mask the whole time. He gave me two vials, one for me and one for Nikki. It was all very illegal, but that made me believe him all the more. Miguel was a by-the-book kind of guy. He followed the rules, and he was breaking some very big ones doing this."

Jaylen rubbed his beard again, not bothering to wipe the tears from his face this time. "So I took the vials home. I injected myself that night. It knocked me on my ass. I woke up in the middle of the night with chills and barely remembered the next day.

"Nikki was traveling for work and got home two days later when I was finally feeling better. Miguel had told me not to talk about it in any traceable way, so I hadn't told her about the vaccine. It wasn't until she was back in our apartment that I showed it to her.

"She was skeptical too, at first, just like I had been. But she knew Miguel, and we both trusted him. Since I seemed to have fared okay from my dose, she decided to take hers. It didn't hit her as bad as it hit me, but a week later..."

Jaylen choked on a sob, unable to continue. Up until that point, Mel had been in a kind of shock. Her emotions weren't processing, though she knew that eventually there would be anger and hurt and sadness. The anger was closest to the surface, and it was justified. But Jaylen was hurting, and she couldn't ignore that.

She reached over and touched his arm. When he accepted her touch, she scooted closer and embraced him.

She could be mad at him later. She could rage and crash-out later. Tonight, Mel held him as he sobbed on her shoulder. A broken man who had lied to her. This man that she loved. This man who was probably going to break her heart, who was *already* breaking her heart.

"I know I should've told you long ago," he said when he could speak again. "It's just, you seemed to be having a hard time with things when we met."

Mel laughed, a harsh sound that felt too loud for the small cabin. "That's because all this," she gestured around wildly, "has been hard for a long time."

He nodded in understanding. "Yeah, you're right. I know. But you seemed to be having a particularly hard time with things when we first met."

She moved away from him and let out a breathy huff. Then, she recalled how he'd found her sobbing at the broken water pump, and the time she crashed her bike in the rain, and her panic attack at the ski jumps. She thought of all the times he'd asked her if she was okay. He had a point, but it didn't justify how long he'd kept this from her.

"You should've told me sooner," she said and couldn't help but go on to explain herself, though she didn't owe him that. "I've been doing so much better lately. I've been happy." She left out the part where she admitted she was happy because of him, but the unsaid words hung in the air.

"Me too. I've been so happy here with you." He reached down to take her hand, but she tucked it under her legs. "And that became the next reason not to tell you. I haven't been this happy with anyone since Nikki, maybe not even then. I love being here in the mountains with you. I didn't want to ruin it."

Mel's chest felt too light and her head ached harder than ever, and it made it hard to breathe. "I...I..." she started, but there was nothing for her to say.

Jaylen rubbed his beard, the skin around his eyes

crinkling in distress. "I'm sorry, Mel. I'm so sorry. I never want to leave you, but I have to."

CHAPTER 34

The numbness that had been keeping Mel's emotions in check was beginning to wear off, and with that, anger rose within her. All this time, Jaylen let her think that he believed they were the only two survivors in the world. While she had no right to his trauma, she felt she had some right to know this fundamental fact of there being a whole community of people out there.

At one time, she had assumed there were other survivors. When she had first come to the cabin, sick with grief and experiencing symptoms of the virus, she thought she was going to die. But then she didn't.

The first time she left the cabin in need of food, she wore a mask to protect herself from germs. She expected to encounter other people, or at least see signs of life. But there were none. Having no idea the level of extinction that had occurred, she gathered her supplies and went back to the cabin until she needed more. Each time she ventured out, she thought this would be the time she'd see another person.

At that point, there wasn't a thought in her head that she was the only one left.

The longer time went on and the more places she

explored, the more she realized how devastating the virus had been. But after that car ride to Virginia, she had convinced herself that if there were any survivors, they were too far away for her to find them—or for them to find her. She had resigned herself to essentially being the only one left, and had vowed to have a self-sustaining existence.

She couldn't help but wonder if she had taken a slightly different route on that fateful trip if she would've ended up in Washington D.C. She might have come across Jaylen and his community.

He should have told her sooner. And now he was going to leave. A sardonic laugh escaped her, one that wasn't like her usual laugh at all.

His eyes were red when he looked at her and his voice was hoarse when he said, "What is it?"

"Nothing." She bit her bottom lip.

He sat up and caressed her hair, his face the saddest she had ever seen it. She missed his bright smile already.

"You're mad at me," he said. "You have a right to be."

All she did was nod. She didn't even know what she wanted to say or how to process any of this. Being angry wasn't going to change what was real. Maybe understanding better where he was coming from might help her figure things out.

"What happened after...?" she trailed off, not wanting to be insensitive.

He finished the question for her. "After Nikki died?"

She nodded again.

He sighed and told her how Miguel never took the vaccine himself but shared all 100 vials with people he knew, some of whom he loved and others whom he thought could help put the world back together. Before Miguel died, he wrote a list of all the people who had the vaccine and gave it to Jaylen.

After Nikki died and enough time had passed where Jaylen thought it was safe, he went in search of all the people on the list and tracked them down. Obviously, not everyone had survived, but some had.

"Us survivors," he said. "We worked on building a community. A year or so ago, two people showed up at our settlement. They were the first survivors we'd met who hadn't taken the vaccine. It made us wonder if there were others out there. We held a meeting and shared ideas. We decided to send four of us out—that's how many solar trucks we had managed to build. I volunteered to go north. And that's how I ended up here with you."

The words "us" and "we" coming out of his mouth had such a different meaning now. Before it had meant Mel and Jaylen, and now it was describing something Mel was not a part of.

The two of them sat next to each other on the bed in silence, the inches of distance between them seeming like a gulf that could not be crossed.

Finally, Jaylen pleaded, "Mel, talk to me. Please."

"I…" she began, but she didn't know what to say. Her mind was somehow swimming with thoughts and yet blank at the same time. She settled on the thing she couldn't get past. "I still don't understand why it took you so long to tell me."

"My plan was always to tell anyone I met right away. But when I first saw you, you were so upset. It didn't feel like the right time. Then, I got focused on fixing the water pump. I almost told you that night at the library, but I chickened out." He rubbed his beard and hung his head. "It never felt like the right time, especially after you told me you thought we were the only people left. The longer I left it, the harder it became to tell you, until I left it entirely too long. And then it felt impossible."

Tears were rolling down his cheeks, only this time they were silent, no heaving sobs to go along with them.

"I was going to tell you everything when I told you about the truck. But I chickened out again. Then, there was the first night we spent together, after the bear. That night, I thought maybe I shouldn't go back. Maybe I should just stay with you. If I did that, I would never have to tell you about the community. But I didn't know if you wanted me to stay that long, and not ever telling you wouldn't have been right either. You deserved to know the truth, the whole of it, whether I stayed here with you or not."

Mel's eyes were dry, but there was a tightness to her chest that made it hard to breathe.

"But you can't," she said. "You can't stay here with me, I mean."

"No. I'm sorry." He wrapped his arms around himself as if he were cold, where Mel only felt overly warm. "I have an obligation to them. They're my community, my family. I've already been gone way longer than I was supposed to be."

"I understand." She really did. She had never expected to keep him for long.

"No, you don't." He cupped her chin in his hand, her eyes raising to meet his. "I want to be with you. I want you to come back with me. I love you, Mel."

Chapter 35

The words "I love you" hung in the room, heavy as the air before a thunderstorm. Mel pulled her chin away from Jaylen's hand. The bed had grown uncomfortably warm, so she scooted closer to the edge of the bed toward the open window. The stagnant summer air outside provided no relief.

Mel loved Jaylen. She'd known that for awhile now, even if she hadn't been able to admit it to herself until very recently. Knowing he loved her in return made this all the more difficult.

"Is that what the others would want?" she asked. "For me to come back with you?"

"Yes," he said. "Our plan is to invite anyone we find into our community. But only if they want to come. We aren't going to force anyone, though there were a few who thought all remaining humanity should come together because it's our only chance of rebuilding any kind of sustainable population."

Mel's stomach twisted uncomfortably at the thought of being forced to go down to D.C. Not that she would be able to do anything to rebuild the population, which Jaylen knew. Being regarded for her reproductive status in such a way made her nauseated enough that she thought she might throw up all over the bed.

"But, Mel," Jaylen continued. "You can stay here if that's what you want. I see how special you've made this place. It's really impressive what you've done here."

"Do you think I should stay?"

He opened his mouth but quickly closed it. What he said next felt carefully worded. "Each person needs to make their own choices. And I don't care about repopulating the world. I'm more concerned about taking care of the people that are here now."

She wasn't sure if he meant all the people here on this earth or if he meant the two of them here in the room. Or perhaps he meant both.

After all, taking care of her was the thing he had done from the moment they had met each other. It was pretty much all he had ever done since she'd known him, and he was very good at it. She imagined all the ways he probably took care of the people of his community. His family, as he had called them; she wasn't sure where that left her.

She took a few shaky breaths, but it failed to settle her emotions or her churning stomach. She closed her eyes and sought out the familiar sounds of the night outside the cabin. The rustle of leaves and the steady rhythm of the crickets were there, but they offered little comfort. And closing her eyes only made her head swim.

Jaylen's hand touched hers and his skin felt icy against hers.

"Are you cold?" she asked, opening her eyes to get a good look at him, only to find her vision was slightly blurred. "We can heat up the stove."

"No, I'm fine."

He pressed her hand in between his as if checking to see

if she was cold. She flinched when pain lanced up her arm. He turned her hand over to discover a puffy, red wound on her palm that was oozing a bit.

"What happened here?" he asked.

Mel fought through the fuzziness in her mind to remember. "A thorn. I pricked it with a thorn."

Concern creased his forehead. He pressed the back of his hand to her forehead. "You're burning up."

"I'm okay."

Not wanting him to have to take care of her again, she jerked away from his touch. The movement made her stomach roll, and she broke out into a cold sweat. She was going to be sick.

Mel shot out of bed and listed sideways with the wave of dizziness that struck her upon standing up so quickly. Bumping off the wall and nearly falling, Mel stumbled her way to the bathroom, making it just in time to lift the lid and throw up in the toilet.

The wood floor was cool on her cheek as she collapsed and rested her face against it. Her stomach lurched, and she shot up to once again empty her stomach in the toilet. This time, Jaylen was there to hold her hair back. When she was done, her head rested in his lap instead of on the floor.

She threw up several more times, the time in between each growing longer until there was nothing left to purge. He gently rubbed her back and mercifully stayed quiet. A headache grew from her temples to encompass her entire skull.

She didn't recall leaving the bathroom, but at some point, she woke up and found herself in bed. Her body was stiff. No sooner had she moaned than Jaylen was by her side.

He helped her sit up and handed her a pink pill. "Take this."

Her body was so weak, she promptly dropped the medicine. He swiped it from the bed and instructed her to open her mouth. When she did so, he popped the pill on her tongue and help a cup of water to her mouth. She managed to choke it down.

"Two more." Jaylen held out his palm to show her two white pills.

Acetaminophen, she recognized, as she swallowed one at a time. For a fever. That was what was making her feel so awful. And the pink one was an antibiotic. For infection.

Blearily, she realized Jaylen must have raided her emergency stock of medicine. The pills were all expired, but hopefully they would work. The cut from the thorn must have gotten infected. She should have taken better care of it. She knew better than to let a wound fester.

She groaned as Jaylen helped her lay back down. Her skin felt hot all over, but her insides were chilled. She shivered under a blanket, while he mopped her forehead with a cool washcloth.

In this instance where she had failed at taking care of herself, Jaylen was once again here to take care of her. Her last thought before she fell into a restless sleep was, *What am I going to do without this man?*

CHAPTER 36

Luckily, the antibiotics worked. Mel's fever burned off as she slept the day away, only stirring periodically for Jaylen to give her medicine and water.

At some point in the night, she woke to a dark room, Jaylen sleeping over the covers. He was facing her but was all the way on the opposite edge of the bed. She couldn't help but think that he was already halfway out of her life.

She also couldn't muster the energy to be angry at him for waiting so long to tell her the truth of where he came from. It was an enormous lie of omission, but she also understood how hard it was to share big truths. Like her fever, the anger had burned away as she slept, and all that was left was a deep well of sadness.

She stretched and took stock of her body. Her skin was sticky, probably from sweating out the fever, and her body was achy. Other than that, she felt okay. Not strong, but her stomach had settled and she was able to light a candle and get to the bathroom by herself.

The bobbing shadows of the candle cast Mel in a strange light when she caught sight of her reflection in the mirror. They heightened the hollows under her eyes and gave her features a haunted look. She placed the back of her hand on her pale forehead to find it cool to the touch. Her mind was no longer trapped in a fog.

She pulled off the bandage that Jaylen must have affixed on her wound while she slept. It was red and slightly puffy, but there was no discharge and it was less tender to the touch. She left it unbandaged, so she could apply aloe to it, like she should've done when the thorn first pierced her skin.

Jaylen was stirring when she came back into the main room of the cabin. She watched him in the dim light from the candle. He felt around on the bed to find it empty next to him. He turned, looking worried, until he spied Mel standing there watching him.

He smiled that big smile of his. "You're up."

She nodded and set the candle on the table. He came over to her and kissed her forehead. His hands rested on her arms, a steadying presence as she looked up at him.

He studied her face. "How're you feeling?"

"Better."

He pulled her close into an embrace. "You had me worried."

"I'm sorry," she whispered.

Her stomach grumbled embarrassingly loud in the quiet of the night.

"Let me get you something to eat."

"It's the middle of the night," she protested.

He studied her face once more. "Are you tired? Do you want to go back to bed?"

She shook her head. They needed to talk, and she was hungry.

He guided her to the couch and draped the throw blanket over her legs. With one more kiss on the forehead, he took the candle into the pantry to see what there was. She stared into the embers of the wood stove, while Jaylen filled the cabin with chatter in that deep voice of his.

"My mom always used to give me saltine crackers and ginger ale when I was sick." She heard him rummaging around in the pantry. "None of that around these days. My mom was so old school, she would use that brown iodine stuff on all my cuts. Boy did that burn! Though, I suppose it did kill the germs. Could've used some of that on your hand."

Mel glanced up briefly as he reemerged without the candle but with his hands full of food containers. Her gaze returned to the embers as she listened to him bang around the kitchen, getting dishes and utensils and turning the water on. She was starting to feel a little sleepy again, listening to his voice as he told more stories of his childhood, his accent more pronounced than usual. She closed her eyes and let his deep voice lull her into a relaxed daze.

"Here you go," he said from startlingly close.

Her eyes popped open to find him holding out a plate of various fresh produce, a pile of nuts, and a thin slice of cornbread. She took it and looked around blearily, following Jaylen's figure as he headed for the kitchen area. It was lit by several candles now, and the wood stove had a couple of fresh logs on it. She must have dozed off.

She turned her attention back to the food and took a small bite of cornbread. It was a bit dry, but she was happy to take another bite to fill her stomach. It was a good sign she had an appetite.

The clink of a glass and running water came from the kitchen. She was trying to eat slowly, letting the food settle to make sure it would stay down. Jaylen set the kettle on the stove and sat next to her. He had his own plate of food and a glass of water.

They sat in their companionable quietness and ate. It was almost like things were completely normal. Like Jaylen had never revealed they were not the only two people left in the world. Like he hadn't confessed he was from a whole settlement of people. Like he hadn't confirmed Mel's worst fear that he was going to leave her. So definitely *not* normal.

The whistle of the teakettle brought Mel back to the present. Jaylen went about making her a tea, presenting it to her with pride when it was ready.

"I hope it's good," he said. "You should drink it all. You're probably dehydrated."

She took a sip obligingly. It was an interesting blend that was a touch bitter, but it was delightfully warm and helped wash down the dryness from the cornbread. While she nibbled her snacks and sipped her tea, Jaylen inhaled all of his food. She wondered if he had been too preoccupied with taking care of her to eat.

"I'm sorry I didn't take better care of my wound," she said once her food was almost gone.

"Hey." He nudged her chin with his finger to turn her face towards his. "It's not your fault. These things happen. Just make sure to finish off that course of antibiotics."

Her eyes filled with tears.

"Hey." He caressed her cheek. "You'll be okay."

It wasn't the infection that had her worried; it was losing him.

"I...we..." She swallowed and found her mouth was dry, so she finished off her tea. "We should talk."

He quickly swiped the plate from her hands, stacked it on top of his empty one, and placed them both on the floor. Then, he pulled her in for a hug.

"Yes, we should," he said into her hair. "But not tonight. Let's get some more rest and we'll talk in the morning."

They settled back into bed, Mel on her side with Jaylen spooning her. She sank into his body, relishing every moment she had left with him.

CHAPTER 37

After sleeping in later than usual, Mel spent the early morning sitting in an Adirondack chair near the chicken coop, sipping a warm tea. With the fever gone and her body rested, she was recovering her strength, and the wound was healing nicely with proper treatment.

Jaylen insisted he feed the chickens and leave food out for the crows. The latter were nowhere to be seen as they had yet to warm up to Jaylen. Crows required time to build up trust, and he hadn't been around long enough to gain it. With a sad resignation, Mel supposed he never would earn their trust.

She wondered what her life would be like after Jaylen left. She hadn't told him she wouldn't be going with him back to D.C., but he had to suspect as much. He was the one who had pointed out how special her cabin home was.

Life had been fine before him; it would go on after he was gone. But it wouldn't be the same. She felt like she had truly started living again after Jaylen had come into her life, and she wasn't sure how to do more than survive without him.

She sighed into her tea mug, glad Jaylen was too far

away to hear her. She didn't want to make him feel guilty about leaving her. He'd already stayed longer than planned.

When Jaylen finished the chore, he came over and sat in the other Adirondack chair. He let out his own sigh, though his sounded contented, not sad.

"I suppose we should have that talk." His gaze pierced hers with more seriousness than she was accustomed to seeing from him.

"I can't come with you," she said quickly, yanking the bandage off rather than peeling it away slowly.

"I said I wouldn't make you."

"You did." She set her empty mug on the big armrest of the chair.

A caw had her looking to the trees. Two big crows sat high atop one of the branches. It was a caw that sounded friendly, not alarmed. They glided to the ground where Jaylen had scattered pieces of the leftover pancakes he had made for breakfast.

One cautiously hopped over to it and grabbed a piece. It took its bounty and alighted upon a low branch of a maple tree. The other crow did a similar hop-step to the food and stole its own piece before heading for the same branch. How could she ever leave this place she loved where she had survived against all odds?

"I won't make you," Jaylen repeated, pulling her attention away from the crows. "But until I leave, I swear I'm going to keep trying to convince you to willingly come with me."

"I'm not sure you can do anything to convince me."

Aside from not wanting to leave her home, Mel was also terrified to go. The thought of such a big change at this point in her life and of meeting all those new people, it was beyond comprehension. Maybe one day she would visit Jaylen—and he was certainly welcome to visit her any time—but to go there forever with him, it was out of the question. Besides, who would take care of her garden and chickens if she left?

"I'll stay until I'm done with your truck," he conceded. "Then I really have to go."

He stood, kissed her on the forehead, and let the topic go for now. She was glad to see him back to his usual, more playful self.

When she went to stand, he shooed her back into her chair. "Relax for today. I'll take care of the chores."

"I'm fine, really."

"I insist."

She shrugged. The more chores he had to do, the longer it would take him to finish the truck.

While Jaylen watered the gardens, picked the ripe produce, and cleaned the henhouse, going so far as to replace the old wood shavings with new ones, Mel sat in the shade and read. Feeling nostalgic and in need of a comfort read, she turned to *Anne of Avonlea*, her favorite of the series. It was one of the few books she had taken from the library to keep in her personal collection at the cabin.

She also had well-worn copies of the books back at her old house, but she had no desire to ever go back there again. So she spent the day lost in the pages of a permanently borrowed book.

When she had her fill of reading, she decided to go all out on dinner. It would be their first proper meal in days and she wasn't sure how many dinners they had left together, so she would put extra effort in for this meal.

In the kitchen, she diced tomatoes, peppers, onions. They all went into a pan with crushed garlic and a pinch of her precious supply of salt. She washed carrots and shaved off thin pieces with the peeler, mimicking something close to linguine in size. As the tomatoes cooked, she blanched the carrots, tossing them into the sauce with a finish of fresh herbs. It wasn't pasta, but it was as close as she had come to it in the after-times.

A crusty French bread would have completed the meal, but she settled for sliced cornbread lightly toasted on each side.

The meal prep tired her a little, but she tried not to show it as she presented the meal to Jaylen on the porch.

He put his face right up to the steam coming off his plate. "This smells amazing. Thank you, Mel."

She handed him a mug of vodka. "No, Jaylen. Thank you for everything you've done around here. With the extra chicken coop, the rain barrels, and the root cellar, I'll be in good shape this winter for anything that comes my way."

"You know," he said around a mouthful of carrots, "down in D.C., we were set to have a decent crop of wheat coming in this fall. Wouldn't it be nice to have something other than cornbread?"

She raised an eyebrow at him, and he backtracked. "Not that this isn't delicious." He dipped the toasted cornbread in the sauce, took a bite, and let out a satisfied noise.

She had tried her hand at growing wheat once. Some kind of blight or fungus or bug had gotten to the plants, so she'd ended up with very little when it came to harvest time. What she had managed to salvage was arduous to process and yielded so little actual wheat flour that she swore off ever growing it again.

"Bread will not entice me." She held firm on not being persuaded, despite her daydreams of real pasta and bread that didn't contain any corn products.

"What about cheese?" He smiled widely.

"Do you have cheese?" she asked, despite her

convictions.

"No, ma'am."

That got her to smile. "I didn't think so."

A small part of her had hoped maybe they did have cheese. She admitted to herself, that might have enticed her. She shook her head as she took the last bite of faux pasta. No, this was home and this was where she belonged.

Chapter 38

All too soon, the dreaded day came when Jaylen pulled up in a truck Mel had never seen before. It was afternoon and she was out in the garden when the tell-tale sound of tires on the dirt driveway announced his arrival. She emerged from the sunflower garden where the stalks were approaching Mel's height, to the abrupt sight of Jaylen stepping out of a red pickup instead of his black one.

Her heart stuttered as he beamed at her.

He waved her over. "Come and see!"

She understood his enthusiasm. Creating a working solar vehicle was an amazing feat, but she was having trouble disguising her reluctance to celebrate such a thing when it meant his departure was imminent.

She managed a smile and a weak "wow" as he showed off the truck like it was his newborn baby. He walked her around it, pointing out different parts and explaining some of the adjustments he'd made. She nodded a lot and murmured generic encouraging sounds.

"Wait until you see my favorite part." He opened the driver's side door with a flourish. "Look inside the center console."

Without being able to imagine anything that would boost her enthusiasm for the truck, Mel hopped inside and opened the console. She stared at the electronic device that sat inside, not quite understanding what she was looking at. It was black and square. At first she thought it might be an external hard drive, but it was a little bigger than she remembered them being. And why exactly would she need a hard drive when there weren't any working computers anymore?

"Plug it in," Jaylen instructed.

Mel looked at him with confusion, so he took the device out and plugged it in below the screen on the dashboard. "It goes right into the USB port here. Turn the car on, I'll show you."

Still confused, she continued to stare at him.

"It's a push start," he said. "Just like mine."

She located the button to start the car and pushed it, while Jaylen rummaged around in the center console.

"Ah, here's the one." He brandished another item that took a minute for Mel to recognize.

It was a CD case of all things. Something she hadn't seen in a long time, but at least she knew what it was. She caught a quick glimpse of the black-and-white photo on the cover before he took out the CD and fed it into the electronic device, clueing Mel in on the fact that it was a CD player.

Jaylen pushed a few buttons, and "Cardigan" by Taylor Swift filled the car.

"Oh!" Her hand went to her mouth. It had been so long since she'd heard recorded music that she almost didn't believe what was happening.

It was entirely different than when she had first heard Jaylen play it on his guitar. That was something new, even when he was covering the same song. Listening to the CD was like a time capsule, bringing her back to a time when it would've played on the radio.

Getting lost in the past was something Mel tried never to do these days. It was too sad, too overwhelming. It was hard to come out of that feeling and face the reality of her current life. It was dangerous. With her emotions already on high alert, she couldn't handle anything that would enhance them.

She didn't bother trying to find a stop button, instead yanking the cord out of the port. She pushed open the door and practically sprinted from the truck, but not before she caught a glimpse of Jaylen's crestfallen face.

Mel rushed into the cabin and slammed the front door shut behind her. Her breaths came in short pants as she slid down the inside of the door to sit on the floor. Once she had her breathing under control, guilt crept in. Jaylen had tried to do this nice thing of keeping music in her life. Her actions came off as totally ungrateful, which she wasn't. She just couldn't handle the music right now.

She blew out a long breath and stood. It was a little early, but she decided to start dinner. As she sliced zucchini and green tomatoes and breaded them with cornmeal in her version of zucchini fries and fried green tomatoes, she decided she would thank him for the truck and the CD player. She didn't need to explain her behavior. He was going to be out of her life before long anyway.

While the vegetables baked, Mel cracked six eggs into a bowl and vigorously beat them. They were good and foamy by the time she poured them into the hot skillet. Once the eggs were done, she split them between two plates, garnished them with freshly sliced green onions, and added the veggies on the side.

Jaylen was waiting for her on the porch when she

emerged from the cabin with dinner in hand.

"Hey," he said and paused as if leaving it open for her to say what was on her mind.

All she did was hand him a plate. He made a few attempts to start a conversation while they ate, but Mel only offered him nods or one-word answers in reply.

He was leaving her; she didn't owe him conversation. She didn't owe him anything. Despite knowing that, her cold treatment of him left a hollow feeling in her stomach. She left her half-eaten dinner sitting in her lap and stared out across the driveway where it was still light enough to see her new truck.

"You going to finish that?" He stood, his plate now empty.

"I'm not hungry." She refused to look at him. "You can have it."

He knelt in front of her and put his plate on the ground. He didn't touch her but was close enough for her to feel his warmth.

"What can I do for you?" he whispered.

She wanted to tell him he could stay with her, give her some time to adjust to the idea that there were other people in the world. Give her time to maybe feel ready to leave her home and join a community of complete strangers. But she didn't know how long that would take, or if she'd ever get to that point.

"Nothing."

"Nothing?" The agony in his voice was palpable. The same deep voice that had broken into Mel's life at one of her most desperate moments. The one that had brought her back from panic more times than she liked to admit. The one that had whispered in the night of a painful past. The one that had made a love confession.

It was also the voice that had lied to her, and the one that would be leaving soon. She looked down into his deep brown eyes, his gaze searching hers to try and figure out how he could help her. She had thought she could start to ice him out of her heart, but it still beat for him and she had no desire to force it not to.

Her throat was tight and she swallowed before saying, "Play for me."

"Really?" That strong voice of his broke over the word.

She nodded. He jumped up and banged through the cabin door, returning less than a minute later with his guitar. He took it out of the case and strummed out a couple of chords.

"I learned a new song for you. I haven't had a lot of time to practice, but I want to play it tonight."

Mel recognized the song after only a few notes, before he even began singing. It was "Crazy Little Thing Called Love" by Queen. She often felt emotional when he played, especially the songs his mom used to sing for him. But tonight, to this song Jaylen had learned for her, there were no words for the feelings spilling over. She was sobbing by the time he reached the chorus.

When he finished, he rushed over to her and pulled her out of the chair into his arms. "I can't tell whether you loved it or hated it."

"Mmmhmm," she said in agreement. When she was able to, she looked up at him, tears still flowing from her eyes. "It was amazing. Better than anything Freddie Mercury could have done, no offense to him."

He leaned down to kiss her long and slow. When he broke the kiss and leaned his chin on her head, all she could think about was how she was going to survive without this man in her life.

CHAPTER 39

A few nights later, Mel woke in the middle of the night, startled and sweating. At first, she thought her fever was back, but then she remembered the nightmare. Not the specifics of what was happening but the feeling of it. Panic. At losing something.

Looking over at Jaylen sleeping next to her and remembering that he was leaving for D.C. in the morning was all the explanation she needed for why she'd had a nightmare like that.

As quietly as she could, she slipped out of bed to go the bathroom. She splashed cold water on her face and patted her neck with wet hands. When she came back, she found Jaylen sitting on the bed, flipping through a book.

She froze when she saw what book it was. "Where'd you find that?"

He held it up, the shiny cover glinting in the lowlight of the embers in the stove. "It was under the bed. I saw it the other day when I was looking for my sock."

Mel said nothing, staring stonily at the book. There was a reason she kept that particular book under the bed. She couldn't let it go, but it was too unfathomably sad to have out on the bookshelf.

"I'm sorry," he said. "I should've left it alone."

"Why?" It came out as a croak, so Mel cleared her throat. "Why didn't you?"

"I wanted to understand why it was under there. It's the only picture book in the cabin. And you were a kindergarten teacher, so I figured it was important, even if it was under the bed. I wanted to know about it before..."

"Before you leave tomorrow," she filled in for him.

"Yes," he said quietly. "I can't know all the little pieces of you, but I want to know as many as I can."

She slid into the bed next to him. "Did you read it?"

He shrugged sheepishly. "I only looked at the pictures."

"Let me have it," she said gently and took it from him.

She lit the candle by the bedside, so she could see the words, though she suspected she could have recited it from heart. It had been more than five years since she had last read this book aloud, but she knew it like no other piece of literature.

"I used to read this on the first day of school to my kindergartners. So they would know that they weren't alone in feeling nervous or sad or scared about the first day of school. We'd do a craft that they would bring home to their parents. So that their grown-ups would know that they weren't alone in being nervous or sad or scared on their kiddo's first day of school."

"Oh." Jaylen sniffed loudly. "That's quite beautiful."

"Do you want me to read it to you?"

He nodded and sniffed again. She focused on the book instead of the tears forming in his eyes.

"This story is called *The Kissing Hand* by Audrey Penn, illustrated by Ruth E. Harper and Nancy M. Leak," she began, just like she was reading it to her class.

Her voice maintained its school reading voice, though a lump formed in her throat on the first page. Tears obscured her vision by halfway through the book where Mrs. Raccoon explains what the kissing hand is to young Chester raccoon. Mrs. Raccoon opens Chester's hand and plants a kiss on his palm. She tells him that whenever he's lonely, he can press his hand to his cheek and feel his mom's love.

At this part, more tears than she thought possible slipped down Mel's face. As she suspected, her memory was strong and she didn't need to see the words to remember them. By the time she got to the end, Jaylen's shoulders were shaking with sobs.

"That was…" he couldn't finish.

He didn't need to say anything more. *The Kissing Hand* was a way to bridge a gap between a separation. For her students, it wasn't a long separation, though it could feel long to them and their parents. For she and Jaylen, well, their separation would be longer, maybe even permanent.

They held each other and cried until they had no more tears. They didn't talked the night away like they had done so many nights before. No, they simply held each other quietly, occasionally murmuring sweet platitudes.

They stayed awake until the morning light began to creep into the cabin and the rooster crowed. It was time to start one of the saddest days of a life that had already seen too many sad days.

Looking up from her spot on Jaylen's chest, she found that he had fallen asleep. She snuck out of his arms and quietly went about her chores. She stoked the fire and filled the kettle with water. She took stock of the prepared food and decided what to feed the chickens and crows this morning.

Instead of their usual simple breakfast, Mel would

make eggs and potatoes—one last hearty meal for them to share.

Jaylen continued to sleep, and she took a moment to take in his peaceful face. His deep umber skin was unlined, his beard was trimmed neatly, and his hair was a bit unruly from sleep. His eyelids fluttered, and she wondered if he was dreaming. If so, she hoped it was a good dream, not a nightmare like she'd had. She wasn't close to having her fill of him when she turned away to face the day.

She put on her boots and headed outside to feed the birds. The sun was working its best to take the chill out of the mountain air, a tease of fall to come, though it felt like summer had just begun. Her boots stomped through dewy grass as she looked over her land, her home. Where, soon, she'd be alone again. Her heart squeezed with longing, and she, once again, considered leaving. But she couldn't. Not right now. Maybe not ever.

When she went back inside with her basket full of eggs, Jaylen was awake and dressed. His backpack and guitar sat by the door, ready for him to take on his journey. When he looked up and saw her, he let loose that big grin of his that made her heart skip a beat.

She held up the basket. "Breakfast before you go?"

He dipped his head and gestured with his hand as if tipping a hat. "That sounds delicious, ma'am."

She had no smile for the joke, all her emotions tied up inside her, not daring to come out. Not yet, not while he was still here.

Jaylen helped her peel and chop the potatoes as the pan heated up. Eggs went on one side, potatoes on the other. Everything was seasoned with fresh herbs.

They sat on the porch and ate slowly, not ready to say goodbye but knowing the time had finally come.

<h1 style="text-align:center">CHAPTER 40</h1>

As Mel watched Jaylen pack up the last of his belongings into his truck, a tight sensation grew in her chest. She felt detached from the moment, an odd haze taking hold of her. There was no fever to blame it on this time.

Her last minutes with Jaylen were slipping away under a brain fog, and there was nothing she could do to stop it. Before she knew it, he was wrapping her up in a hug, his face tucked into the hair on top of her head.

She heard him breathe in deeply before straightening. He offered her no words of comfort. Instead he held one of her hands in his and placed it palm up. He kissed her palm and folded her fingers over it, just like in *The Kissing Hand*.

That lifted the fog and grounded her in the moment. She returned the gesture. Now they would always have a kiss from each other when they needed it, no matter how far apart they were. With the haze gone, tears pushed against the back of her eyes, but she didn't want to cry right now so she held in the sobs.

She buried her face into Jaylen's chest for one last hug, breathing him in as he had done to her earlier. Finally, she reached up to cup his face, raised up on her tippy-toes, and kissed him. When they broke apart, they stared at each other, Mel losing herself in those deep brown eyes.

They didn't say goodbye. Jaylen simply got into the truck and rolled down the window. She stood a few feet away,the tightness spreading from her chest into her throat. Sticking his arm out the window, he waved the whole time as the truck slowly made its way to the end of the driveway. He turned right at the road, so Mel could no longer see him. Then, the truck was gone, lost behind the trees lining the road.

She pressed the hand he had kissed to her cheek and found it was cold. There was no holding back the sobs. She stumbled back to the cabin, through the door, and collapsed onto the bed. She lay there for what felt like a long time, but what did time mean anymore?

Without Jaylen, time would spread out in an endless cycle of days, the monotonous chore of staying alive the only thing left. He had shown her how to live, but now she wasn't sure she could do that without him. She was back to just surviving.

The next second.

The next minute.

The next hour.

After an indeterminate amount of time swallowed in grief as bad as the early days of her isolation, Mel shook herself loose of the tangle of blankets on the bed. She forced herself to get up and into the bathroom where she splashed water on her face and arms. She lightly slapped her cheeks to snap herself back into reality.

This was no way to exist. What was she clinging to here on this mountainside all alone?

The crows would survive without her. She could figure out a way to get the chickens to D.C. if she tried. She could bring her seeds and herbs there, too. Right?

Her resolve faltered as she stared at her reflection in the dingy bathroom mirror. Figuring all of that out would've been so much easier if Jaylen had still been there. That was it!

She would go find him. He couldn't have gotten too far away. She packed her bags with supplies and a couple of changes of clothes, and then mapped out a route on the atlas. Jaylen would probably head east to the main highway that would take him south toward New York City.

How many miles did he say the truck could go on a full charge of sunlight? She couldn't remember, but it didn't matter. She would find him even if she had to drive all the way to Washington, D.C.

Once outside, she left her bags on the porch and noticed the sun was past its peak, so that meant afternoon. This time of year, that would still give her quite a few hours before sunset. If she drove as far as the charge would take her into the night and woke up early in the morning, hopefully she could catch him in a couple of days.

She went to the chicken coops and threw extra bread, lentils, and seeds into them, hoping the birds wouldn't eat it all in one day. In the garden, she picked a handful of ripe tomatoes and peppers and put them in a basket to take with her. With the backpack on and her arms weighed down with the basket and other bags, she made her way out to her truck.

A puff of dirt at the end of the driveway froze her in her tracks. She watched in shock as Jaylen's truck drove down the driveway and stopped in front of her. He wore that radiant smile of his as he exited the vehicle.

Mel was speechless, but that was okay because Jaylen was there.

He gestured to her bags. "Going somewhere?"

"I—" She didn't know how to explain what she was doing.

"You weren't by any chance coming to find me, were you, ma'am?"

She cleared her throat, the basket bobbling precariously on her arm. A tomato tipped over the edge and splatted on the dirt. It was a waste of perfectly good food, a thing Mel would normally care about, but she didn't give it a second thought.

Jaylen took the burdens from her arms and placed them on the ground.

"I needed your help with something," she admitted.

"I thought I did everything for you before I left."

She shrugged. "I guess not."

His grin turned so bright she almost felt like she had to look away. Or maybe she felt that way because his gaze seemed to look right into her, seeing into the deepest parts of her soul.

"Well, I'm here now," he said. "What did you need me to do?"

She opened her mouth to explain about how she wanted his help packing up the things she needed and properly closing down the cabin. But something stopped her. Jaylen was here. Back at her home when he should have been on his way to D.C.

"Wait," she said. "Why are you here?"

"I..." His smile faltered, and he seemed unsure of himself. "I was out on the road all by myself when I realized something."

She waited, but it wasn't long before impatience got the better of her. "What did you realize?"

His gaze had turned distant, like his mind was far away

—maybe back on the road. When it snapped back to Mel, all she felt was tenderness.

"I realized I missed you," he said. "I had barely left, and I missed you. Then, I realized I wasn't ready to leave, not unless you were ready to come with me." He fingered the straps of her backpack. "Are you ready to come with me?"

She quickly said, "Not right now."

"Hmmm," he murmured as he pointedly looked down at the basket and bags he had taken from her and put on the ground.

"I'm not ready," she insisted. "I can't leave the chickens here by themselves for long."

A few minutes ago, she had been ready to recruit Jaylen to help her leave home. But he had come back to her, and that changed things. The possibility of him staying longer was too big a temptation. It would give her time to properly prepare to leave. Or maybe he would permanently change his mind and they wouldn't have to leave at all.

"How long can you stay?" It was a question she had been so afraid of for so long, but now she found it easy to ask.

"I can stay through winter. As long as you have enough supplies. I can hunt more geese and go fishing. I'll even go ice fishing if I have to."

"Why do you think I cleared that extra garden space? I wanted to make sure I had enough for two this winter."

He'd be around to go blueberry picking, to see the sunflowers bloom, and for the first snowfall. She nudged him with her elbow playfully. He grabbed her arm, all seriousness. He gently grasped the back of her head and kissed her like she had never been kissed before.

When they finally came up for air, they held each other for a long time. It was like neither one wanted to let go of the other. They hugged in the driveway as the sun dipped lower and lower.

She was happy to be reunited with him, even though they had only been parted for a short time. It had almost been a very long time, though, and that's what made this moment so special.

"We can celebrate the New Year together," Mel said, her face squished up against his chest. It had been ages since she'd had someone to kiss at midnight.

"Yes," Jaylen said, his voice husky. "We can."

"And then?" she couldn't help asking.

She waited for him to say that he would leave after that. Or for him to say she should go with him to D.C.

Instead, he said, "We'll figure that out when the time comes."

She looked up at him and met his gaze. "Yeah?"

"Yes." He tipped her chin up and pecked her lips. "Is that okay, ma'am?"

It was overkill with the second ma'am since he'd come back, but Mel couldn't help the grin that broke out on her face. "That's okay with me."

She vowed not to think too hard about the future. She would simply enjoy living with this man who had come into her life at a time when she had thought she was the only person left on earth. This man who had changed her, who had taught her what it meant to live instead of just survive. She would enjoy every minute she had with him on this big planet that no longer seemed so lonely.

Mel's Strawberry Rose Water Cornbread Recipe

Ingredients:
- 2 cups cornmeal
- 1/2 tsp salt
- 2 cups water
- 1 tbsp rose water
- 1 tbsp apple cider vinegar
- 4 tbsp maple syrup
- 3 eggs separated
- 1 cup diced strawberries
- honey drizzle

Directions:
1. Preheat oven to 400° F. Line an 8x8 inch baking pan with parchment paper.*
2. In a large bowl, add the cornmeal and salt. Whisk to combine.
3. Create a well in the center of the dry ingredients and add the beaten egg yolks, water, rose water, apple cider vinegar, and maple syrup. Mix to combine.
4. In a separate bowl, whisk the egg whites until they form stiff peaks.
5. Fold in the diced strawberries and the egg whites.
6. Bake for 35-40 minutes until edges begin to brown and a toothpick comes out clean. Let cool for 10 minutes before slicing and serving with a drizzle of honey on top.

*Mel wouldn't have access to butter or bacon grease to keep the cornbread from sticking to the pan. She would likely have a supply of parchment paper, so that's what I use for this recipe. No judgement if you cheat a little and grease the pan instead of using parchment.

About the Author

Award-winning author Katie L. Carroll writes books for kids, teens, and those who are young at heart. She began writing after her 16-year-old sister, Kylene, unexpectedly passed away. Since then, writing has taken her to many wonderful places—both real and imagined. She wrote her YA fantasy ELIXIR BOUND, winner of the 2019 Connecticut Author Project for Best YA, and its sequel ELIXIR SAVED so Kylene could live on in the pages of a book.

If you enjoyed SUNFLOWERS AT THE END OF THE WORLD, be sure to write a review on your favorite book retail sites. Katie's other novels include the YA thrillers BLACK BUTTERFLY: SPY AGENTS, BOOK ONE and ONLY DARK EDGES, and the middle grade books WITCH TEST and PIRATE ISLAND.

Her Family Holiday Tales picture books, illustrated by Phoebe Cho, are MOMMY'S NIGHT BEFORE CHRISTMAS, DADDY'S 12 DAYS OF CHRISTMAS, and GRAMMY'S HALLOWEEN SCARE. She is also the author of the picture book THE BEDTIME KNIGHT, illustrated by Erika Baird, and the nonfiction books SELFIES FROM MARS: THE TRUE STORY OF MARS ROVER OPPORTUNITY and THE GREAT VOYAGERS: EARTH'S INTERGALACTIC AMBASSADORS. She teaches writing and publishing workshops for children and adults and serves on the Library Board for her local public library. Visit her website at katielcarroll.com.

9 781958 575147